WHITE LIGHTNING RUN

Screeching around a bend, Jack dropped the roaring T-bird down to a hundred miles an hour and started the turn. Out of nowhere, his headlights lit up another car parked only a few feet off the side of the road. Jack's eyes were drawn to the symbol on the side of the door. He was moving so fast he couldn't read the lettering, but he didn't have to. It was the North Carolina Highway Patrol, and the man behind the wheel was a state trooper.

"Uh, oh!" whispered Jack as his foot automatically hit the brake and he started to slow down. Then it hit him.

"What the hell am I doing? I'm carrying a hundred gallons of illegal whiskey, doing nearly one hundred miles an hour in a supercharged T-bird . . . And I'm gonna stop?"

Planting his foot on the accelerator, he said, "I don't think so!" And took off like a rocket. . . .

CHECKERED FLAG

Southern Runnin'

JAMES PRUITT

JOVE BOOKS, NEW YORK

SOUTHERN RUNNIN'

A Jove Book / published by arrangement with
the author

PRINTING HISTORY
Jove edition / July 2000

The Penguin Putnam Inc. World Wide Web site address is
http://www.penguinputnam.com

ISBN: 0-515-12805-8

A JOVE BOOK®
Jove Books are published by The Berkley Publishing Group,
a division of Penguin Putnam Inc.,
375 Hudson Street, New York, New York 10014.
JOVE and the "J" design
are trademarks belonging to Penguin Putnam Inc.

PRINTED IN THE UNITED STATES OF AMERICA

10 9 8 7 6 5 4 3 2 1

1

June 15, 1969

It was a hot and sultry June night and the heat of the day still emanated from the concrete and glass maze of the city well after dark. Amid the whining of air conditioners and wonder of television, the people of Charlotte, North Carolina, sought a few hours of relaxation from their hectic daily lives. The day had been a scorcher, and the forecast was for more of the same.

Not so in the western part of the state. Along the regions of the Blue Ridge a cool, almost chilly, breeze moved along the mountains. In a large clearing of one of those mountains, Walker Kincade took a final drag off a cigarette as he watched the last of the moonshine being loaded.

Lonnie "the Bear" Hendricks, a six-foot-six giant of a man who weighed well over three hundred pounds, stepped up to the car. Lonnie was the ramrod for all the liquor-running out of Haywood County. He was the overseer and enforcer for Big Daddy Wilkes, the money man and brains behind most of western Carolina's illegal whiskey-running. He supplied the big cities of North Carolina and occasionally the folks on the other side of the Smokey Mountains.

Leaning in the driver's-side window, Lonnie switched on the ignition key and watched the needle of a special gauge mounted next to the steering column as it swung steadily to the right, indicating that the hundred-gallon stainless steel tank mounted underneath was filled to capacity. He switched off the key and started to step back, then, as an afterthought, he reached down under the driver's seat. His fingers felt around until they came into contact with what he was searching for; the grip of a .45 caliber automatic pistol, mounted just under the front edge of the seat. The weapon was equipped with an ejector spring. When activated, the spring would propel the pistol out from under the seat and straight into the driver's hand.

Satisfied with his inspection, Lonnie stepped back from the car, spit a lethal stream of chewing tobacco through the air and shouted, "You're all set, Walker. Got a full load and ready to roll."

Walker nodded and, slapping the big man on the back, said, "Thanks Lonnie." Opening the door, he slid in behind the wheel. Strapping himself into the bucket seat, Walker made a quick check of the gauges and interior of the modified 1964 Chevrolet. To the everyday driver on the street, the interior of the car would seem no different than the one they owned or saw everyday. But looks could be very deceiving. In order to accommodate the concealed tank required for the whiskey, certain modifications had been made. The passenger-side bucket seat was no more than a shell placed over a high-rise portion of the tank. The rear bench seat was the same: A hollowed-out shell that gave the appearance of a normal seat, but concealed a large portion of raised tank, which extended to a false bottom in the trunk. As much space as possible had been utilized to allow for maximum capacity, while at the same time assuring that the car appeared as normal as any of the other thousands on the street.

Turning the ignition, the Chevy roared to life. Its huge modified 427 engine rumbled like an oversized monster straining to be released from its cage. Allowing the monster to idle, Walker Kincade lit another cigarette. Like a fighter pilot making a preflight check, he began to scan the bank of gauges illuminated in front of him. Oil pressure, rpms, temperature, and manifold pressure. Reaching forward, he flipped on a switch and a police scanner came to life, its trail of blinking lights racing back and forth, searching out any radio traffic in the immediate area.

Placing his foot on the gas pedal he revved the V-8 then let off the gas, then revved her up again. All the time, his experienced eyes watched each of the gauges rise and fall with each acceleration. His left foot depressed the heavy clutch pedal as his right hand dropped to the chrome-balled lever of the Borg Warner, four-speed floor-shift, gear box. Walker began running through the series of gear positions with a smooth precision that exemplified natural ability coupled with experience. Each motion was made with the same sensitivity of a surgeon, his right hand alert for the slightest thing out of the ordinary, a vibration, a catching motion or rough exchange while going from one gear to another. There were no problems. Everything was perfect. And why shouldn't it be—after all, he'd built this car from the ground up. From the screw jack-adjustable, reinforced "A" frames and heavy-duty coils to the differential with floating hubs. Reinforced brake shoes and ventilated drums, to the powerful 427ci, V-8, 427 horsepower motor that could turn 140 miles per hour. Walker Kincade knew this car better than he knew his wife—and both of them were fine . . . very fine.

Lonnie was at the side window again. "Sounds pretty damn good, Walker. How's she lookin'?"

"Hotter'n hell and ready to go prowlin', son. Guess we're as ready as we'll ever be. We got anything comin' back this trip?"

Lonnie the Bear shook his head, slinging a string of tobacco drool on the side door. "Naw, the other boys are pickin' up the sugar and the rest of the fixin's this trip." Lonnie paused, as if double-checking his thoughts to see if he'd forgotten anything, "Naw, can't think of nothin' Walker. Wanta' thank ya' for takin' on this load on such short notice. Woulda' really put my butt in a crack if I hadn't got it outta' here tonight. Don't imagine your wife, Claire, thought mucha' me callin' ya'—her wantin' you to quit and all."

Walker shook his head, "Don't worry about it, Lonnie. Besides, we can use the money with the baby comin' anytime. Reckon I better get on it if I'm gonna' make it to Charlotte before mornin'."

Lonnie's face took on a serious look as he said, "Now Walker, you just remember to watch yourself outside Collinsville. From what I hear, that damn Sheriff Bill Jennings down there really wants your ass after that little tiff you all had on that run a couple months ago. Some folks say he ain't been right in the head since. You sure made him look like a horse's ass."

Walker grinned as he thought of that last encounter and said, "Yeah, that man just ain't got no sense of humor at all. Makes a fellow wonder if maybe his real daddy wasn't a northern boy."

Lonnie laughed, "Jeez, Walker! Jennings might be as low down as a turtle turd—but a damn Yankee! I wouldn't call my worst enemy nothin' that low."

They were both still laughing as Lonnie stepped back

from the car. Sticking his big hands into his coveralls he spit another stream of tobacco a good ten feet as he watched the taillights of the coal black Chevy disappear into the North Carolina night.

Cruising at seventy miles per hour, the well-balanced Chevy took the curves with ease as Walker guided the high-powered machine down the twisting roads that would send him around Collinsville and toward the interstate that would take him into the growing metropolis of Charlotte.

It was a run he had made hundreds of times, but one he always enjoyed. With the pleasant Carolina breeze swirling about him, he lit a smoke and thought about the first time he'd ever made the Charlotte run. He had been thirteen and the driver that night had been his uncle. Waylan Kincade had loaded his nephew into the car amid the wild screams and protests of Walker's mother. "He'll get the boy killed!" she'd shouted as they drove away. But Uncle Waylan had only laughed and answered, "Gotta teach 'em young, Hattie."

With that jewel of wisdom expressed by his uncle, young Walker Kincade had set out on the ride of his life. To this day, Walker wasn't sure if that ride was meant to scare the hell out of him or was simply an uncle trying to impress his nephew with his driving ability, but whatever the old man's reasoning, Walker discovered that there was nothing in the world that could provide the adrenaline rush he experienced like the sound of squealing tires, the roar of a finely tuned engine and most of all, the feeling of speed. Now, twenty years later, the only thing that had changed was the size of the engines, which were getting faster every year.

Lonnie had been right about one thing: Claire hadn't been happy about his decision to make this run. Especially since he had promised her he would get a normal job and give up the 'shine business now that he was going to be a father. He had tried to argue that it was only because of the baby and their need for the extra money that he had given in to Lonnie's request, but Claire knew better. Walker had grown up among moonshiners and fast cars. It was all he knew. In her heart, she doubted she could ever change his love for cars and speed and had reluctantly accepted that fact. It was the illegal liquor-running that really concerned her. The thought of Walker being locked away in a federal prison, never having the chance to spend time with their child—to watch him or her grow into a fine young man or woman. As painful as that would be for her, she knew it would kill Walker. Although she had lost the argument this night, he had promised her this would definitely be his last run . . .

2

There wasn't a cloud in the sky to obscure the bright full moon that night. From his position on the hillside overlooking the highway, Sheriff Bill Jennings studied the terrain. The moonlight reflecting off the road below made the highway appear more like a twisting silver river than a highway, and there was no doubt in the lawman's mind that Walker Kincade would be running flat out down that silver ribbon sometime after midnight with his illegal load of whiskey and this time Bill Jennings was going to be ready for him. There weren't going to be any fuck-ups like last time. He'd made sure of that. Taking a long drag off his cigarette, the lawman's eyes roamed the silver strip as he thought of the numerous times he had pursued "trippers" through these mountains. He'd caught a lot of them over the years, but never the elusive Kincade brothers. There were three of them. Charlie was the oldest, then came Rich, and finally the youngest of the bunch, that damn hot-shot driver, Walker. It was Walker that had been the pain in the ass over the last ten years, costing him more in time, manpower and equipment than all the damn shiners on the mountain.

Tossing the smoke on the ground, Jennings stomped it out with excessive fury as he recalled his last encounter with Walker Kincade on this very highway only four weeks earlier.

The sheriff and his deputies had received a tip that Walker was making a run that night. They had blocked off the road with two patrol cars parked nose to nose. Shortly after midnight they heard the unmistakable deep roar of a powerful engine making its way down the mountain, but there wasn't a light to be seen anywhere. As uneasy minutes passed, the roar echoed through the mountains and valley, coming closer and growing louder, but no one could see a thing.

As the sound bore down on them, the lawmen brought their shotguns over the hoods of their cars and pointed them into the darkness of the highway that stretched out before them. They couldn't see a thing, but something was coming their way, and it was moving damn fast.

Walker's headlights had seemed to appear like magic less than a hundred feet in front of the startled lawmen. The experienced whiskey runner had expected a road-block, but knowing Jennings and his predictability, as well as the highway like the back of his hand, Walker had cut his lights halfway down the mountain. He had backed the big Chevy off to sixty miles an hour and allowed his experienced feel for the road to take over. Rounding Kelly's Bend he had seen the flicker of a cigarette lighter and knew the roadblock lay five hundred feet ahead. Waiting until the very last moment, Walker had flipped on his bright lights.

The element of surprise had been total. Like deer caught in the headlights, the lawmen were momentarily stunned, then scrambled like rabbits to abandon the road-block. Certain that all the men were clear, Walker floored the big Chevy with the steel-reinforced front end. It struck the patrol cars exactly where the two front bumpers touched and sent them spinning like two huge tops to each side of the road, one ending up in a ditch and the other going through a guardrail, rolling end over end, three hundred feet down the side of the mountain.

By the time Jennings and his men picked themselves up off the ground and raised their weapons, there was nothing left to shoot at, only the fading sound of Walker's 427 Chevy, which had disappeared into the darkness of the mountain road.

Sheriff Jennings had seemed to snap at that point. In a rage and out of frustration, he jacked a round into the twelve-gauge shotgun he was carrying, and taking three steps toward his own car which had been parked off the side of the road, he blew the windshield to pieces, all the time cussing the name of Walker Kincade with each round he fired.

The frustration came from the fact that Walker had gone through them like they weren't even there and the knowledge that to try and have the tripper arrested later would be a waste of time. Any damage done to Walker's car would be repaired before the Charlotte police had a chance to locate it. Toss in the fact that it was a dark night, there was no positive I.D. of the driver and no damage to the supposed vehicle involved and it all added up to the sheriff getting an ass-chewing from a judge for wasting his time. Bill Jennings knew the routine by heart—he'd been through it enough to know he'd be pissin' in the wind trying to have Walker Kincade arrested.

With the other two cars totaled, the sheriff's car was the only transportation left back to town. As the deputies were clearing the shattered glass of the windshield from their boss's car, one of the deputies had half-jokingly said, "That damn Walker must have eyes like a fuckin' cat to be runnin' this road blind like that."

"Yeah, an' he must think he has as many lives as a fuckin' cat to be runnin' flat out like that, but damn I gotta' give it to him—he sure as hell can drive," said another.

Lawmen and trippers had been playing out this cat-and-mouse game since the days of Prohibition. But now it was the sixties and even the Feds had pretty much backed off the idea of stopping the illegal running of moonshine whiskey out of the mountains. There were fewer and fewer dry counties left and everyone figured before long you could buy "moon" legal at any liquor store and the days of the trippers would become a thing of the past. Besides, the Feds had their hands full trying to deal with a new problem that was growing faster than illegal whiskey ever did. Drugs had become the new priority—not a bunch of good ol' boys brewin' whiskey in the backwoods.

Amazingly, few people who practiced the trade of running shine had actually been killed outright in confrontations with the law. More had died from car crashes and personal feuds than from the bullets of lawmen. Some folks said Walker was just lucky; others said luck had nothing to do with it. He was just the best tripper to come out of the Blue Ridge Mountains in a long, long time.

But that night, Bill Jennings was hardly impressed with Walker Kincade's reputation. His deputies could tell by the look on the sheriff's face and the tone of his voice that this was no longer a game of cat and mouse. Any misunderstanding of that point vanished as they drove back into town for a tow truck. All the way back Jennings kept repeating the same thing over and over. "I'm going to kill that fucker next time—gonna kill him fuckin' dead. By God, I swear it!"

There was not a man in that patrol car that doubted

what Bill Jennings said. The days of fun and games were over. It had become personal . . . very personal.

Now here they were, four weeks later, waiting for Walker and his coal black Chevy and its illegal load of whiskey. But this time was different. This time they wouldn't be aiming at the tires or the radiator to disable the car. No, this time their orders were clear. They were going strictly for the driver. As an added incentive, Jennings made the threat that if Walker Kincade made it off that mountain alive, there would be three Haywood County deputies without a job come morning.

It was just a little past midnight when one of the deputies came up the hill driving a fully loaded propane tanker. Cutting the wheel to the left slightly, he pulled the truck across the road at an angle, totally blocking the highway. Any attempt to go around the tanker on the right would put the driver into the towering Carolina pines. Any attempt around the left would send the driver through a guardrail and off a cliff that dropped seven hundred feet straight down.

Kneeling down on one knee, Jennings lit a smoke and stared up into the darkness of the mountain from which he knew his prey would soon be coming out of his lair. A slow grin worked its way across his face as he inhaled deeply and spoke to the mountain, "Okay, Walker—let's see you push that fuckin' thing off the road!"

3

Walker was halfway down the mountain now. He could feel the cool night breeze beginning to give way to the warmer air of the flatlands below. Every now and then he would catch sight of the bright moon peeking through the tops of the pines. It was a great night for a run—his last run. He'd already made up his mind about that. This would be his last one. He'd made his promise to Claire and he'd live up to it. After all, everything she had said made sense. And God he hated it when that happened. A fellow could argue with a woman when he thought she was wrong, but it was altogether a different story when even the fellow knew she was right.

He was about to become a father and with that new title came a whole new set of responsibilities. None of which included racing down a mountain at a hundred miles an hour, breaking the law and getting shot at. It was time for Walker Kincade to become a responsible husband and father. To get a respectable job and become a real family man like normal husbands and fathers.

At first the thought of all that had scared the hell out

of him, or maybe it was just the idea of it all coming at
him at once. A father, responsibility, a respectable job,
normal family, a normal life. Hell, all he'd known growing up was moonshine, guns, and fast cars. Now he was
just supposed to let it all go. Disappear, as if it had been
someone else who had lived that life. But when he
thought about it, he wasn't really letting it go—that
lifestyle was going on its own. Time was about to over-
take the moonshine life. It had been a hell of a run in its
heyday, but it was almost 1970, and that lifestyle was
beginning to fade just as the cowboys and great cattle
drives of another era. Claire was right. It was time to
end it.

Walker considered what he was going to do after running this last load. Vern Gasdon had offered him a job as
his top mechanic at the Chevy dealership in Charlotte.
The pay was more than fair. Then there was always the
prize money from dirt track racing. That was, if a fellow
could finish in the top three. Outside of running moon
and working on cars, there was nothing Walker liked
more than racing.

What had started out as a recreational way to kill time
between liquor runs had since evolved into a big-time
sport with the prize money getting bigger and bigger each
year. With his talent and natural skills behind the wheel,
few doubted that Walker could become one of the best in
Darlington or Daytona, hell, even the country, if only
he'd take it serious. He had to admit, it was an idea he
toyed with over the last few months but for now, sliding
around curves at the local dirt tracks, winning a few hundred dollars every now and then, and racing against some
of the good ol' boys he'd grown up with was satisfying
enough. Besides, that hard-top Daytona style racing took
a hell of a lot of money. And a damn sight more than a
grease monkey could afford.

Walker's thoughts were interrupted by something that

caught his eye. He wasn't sure what it was, but for a fleeting second he could swear he saw a flash of moonlight off metal. His mind and body became suddenly alert. "Jennings," he muttered to himself. "Damn. My last run and that asshole can't let it go."

Walker backed the big Chevy off to sixty miles an hour, a good cruising speed, at least until he knew what was going on. On the next switchback curve, Walker caught a glimmer of light off metal again. His first thought was of another roadblock, but he had to give it to Jennings. This time the sheriff had picked the perfect spot. The Turner drop-off on the left and nothing but towering pines on the right. It was a damn good bet that the cars wouldn't be parked hood to hood this time, and if they were, more than likely they'd be chained together under the mainframes. If he tried to split them like last time the cars wouldn't go spinning off the road; instead the chain would swing the cars inward and slam Walker into a high-impact sandwich with no room to maneuver.

Rounding the last curve, Walker's headlights illuminated the huge tanker truck that blocked the road. "Holy shit!" he yelled. "You're one mean machine, baby. But even you ain't movin' that thing off the road."

Thirty yards from the tanker, Walker stomped on the brake and cut the wheel hard left, at the same instant hitting the gas petal. Smoke rolled from the rear tires as the Chevy did a one-eighty in the middle of the road.

"Fire!" screamed Jennings at the top of his lungs, as he brought his shotgun to his shoulder and opened up on the black Chevy. The darkness came alive with the roar of gunfire, buckshot ripping metal, mixed with the sounds of shattering glass and squealing tires, all played out in a kaleidoscope of exploding light from the lethal weapons of the lawmen.

The inside of Walker's car became a deadly metal shell of ricocheting buckshot mixed with flying glass that punctured, ripped and tore the interior to pieces. Walker felt the Chevy shudder as he downshifted and popped the clutch, fighting desperately to get the car out of range of the shotguns. Another hit sent a swarm of pellets off the passenger-side door post and into the dash, shattering the gauges. At the same instant, Walker felt a searing pain rip into his right leg and ankle. He was hit and it hurt like hell.

Back at the roadblock, Jennings was running to his car and screaming, "Get that fuckin' truck outta' there! I've got that bastard this time, by God."

Two of the deputies ran to the sheriff's car, but before they could get in, Jennings punched the accelerator and tore off after Walker, narrowly missing the front of the propane truck that had just begun to move out of the way.

"That son-of-a-bitch is out of his mind!" yelled one of the deputies.

There was a mix of panic and excitement in the voice of another as he shouted, "Come on! We've got to catch up or somebody's gonna' die tonight, sure as hell."

Pausing only long enough to collect the deputy that had moved the truck, the lawmen burnt rubber as their cars whipped out onto the highway in pursuit of Walker Kincade and their overzealous boss.

Walker's leg and ankle were killing him. The slightest movement of the ankle sent a bolt of blinding pain up his leg. There was little doubt in his mind that the ankle was broken. The seat was wet with blood from the hole in his leg located only a few inches above the knee. At least the Chevy was in better shape than he was. It had plenty of holes, but nearly all of the shot had passed through without causing major damage. Luckily Walker had gotten the front end swung around before they opened fire, saving the radiator and engine. The rear window and part of the passenger-side windshield were gone, and stuffing from the riddled dash flew about the interior like a high wind passing through a cotton factory.

Weaving his way back up the mountain, Walker tried to ignore the pain as he lit a cigarette and inhaled deeply before letting it out. A slow smile came over his face as he whispered, "Guess Lonnie was right. That's one pissed-off sheriff."

The moment of tension-relieving humor was short-lived as Walker noticed a flash of headlights in what was left of his rearview mirror. He knew who it was behind him and the bastard was coming on fast.

Walker's pain was overridden by a sudden surge of adrenalin. Hanging the cigarette from the corner of his lips, he glanced up at the mirror. When the approaching lights were within a hundred feet, he downshifted the Chevy and said, "Okay, asshole, let's see what'cha got."

The shattered ankle forgotten for the moment, Walker floored the pedal. The powerful 427 leaped forward, quickly climbing to a hundred and ten miles per hour with the oversize tires straining every thread to hold the big car on the curves.

Bill Jennings had totally lost all sense or reason. He was obsessed with putting an end to Walker Kincade once and for all. Seeing the Chevy lunge forward in the attempt to outrun him, Jennings downshifted the brand new 1969 Ford Torino he had confiscated from the local Ford dealership, claiming it was for official business. Flooring the gas pedal he felt the power of the Ford's 427 engine surge forward and, laughing like a madman, yelled at the top of his lungs, "I've got the horses to keep up with your ass this time, you son-of-a-bitch!"

Walker couldn't believe the lawman was so damn persistent. He was pushing a hundred and twenty-five and Jennings was still with him and closing fast. There was one final curve coming up before they would hit a seven-mile stretch of straightaway. If Walker could keep him off his ass till he hit that straightaway, he had a chance. After all, there was more to fast driving than just a fast car. It was what a man could do with that car that made the difference, and the one thing Walker wasn't short of was guts and confidence in his car or his ability.

The trees and guardrail were a blur as Walker went into the final curve, the Chevy straining to hold the road. A sudden bump from the Torino sent the Chevy into a wild, fish-tailing slide. It took every effort at Walker's command to keep the car on the road. It veered wildly to the left, glanced off the guardrail, the blow sending the car into a slide back across the road to the right, barely missing a massive pine at the edge of the highway. Blinding pain fired through Walker's body as he fought to regain control and somehow managed to bring her out of the slide and back into the middle of the highway at the beginning of the straightaway.

Behind him, Bill Jennings was grinning like a crazy man. He had him now and he knew it. There was no way the Chevy could outdistance the Torino. Stomping the gas pedal, he shot the Ford forward and slammed into the Chevy's rear bumper, causing the car to fishtail again. Backing off a few feet, Jennings repeated the move again, only harder this time. Each impact sent riveting pain through Walker's ankle that quickly spread through his entire body. Adding to the pain was the fact that the amount of blood in the seat had nearly doubled and the blood loss was beginning to take its toll on Walker. He began to experience a sense of weakness in his arms and his vision was blurring off and on. "This whole situation is getting out of hand," he thought.

For a fleeting second, Walker considered backing off the Chevy, pulling over and surrendering to the lawman before somebody got killed. But that thought quickly vanished from his mind as the Torino delivered another bone-shattering slam to the rear of the Chevy. No, this guy wasn't going to be satisfied with slapping the cuffs on him. It'd gone way beyond that, now. As the Ford backed off again and prepared for another strike, Walker cussed under his breath then shouted, "Okay, you dick! Enough is enough—bring it on!"

There was less than four miles of straightaway left. If Walker was going to make his move it had to be now. Eyeing the headlights in his broken mirror, he watched the Ford coming on like an out-of-control freight train. When it was within ten yards of the Chevy's rear bumper, Walker pulled the steering wheel left, then straightened it out, at the same instant stomping down on the brake pedal with all the strength that remained in his left leg. There was the sound of screaming tires and a cloud of smoke as the Chevy fought to come to a stop. The smell of scorched metal from the brake pads and burnt rubber filled the interior of Sheriff Jennings's car as it shot past, sideswiping the right side of the Chevy, sending up a rain of sparks as the Torino tore off the door handles and side mirrors of both cars. The rear bumper of the Ford caught on the right front fender of the Chevy as Jennings's car passed, literally ripping it off and dragging it in a shower of sparks for over thirty yards before coming loose and cart-wheeling end over end off the side of the road and into a ditch.

Everything had happened so fast that by the time Jennings realized what Walker had done, he found himself fifty yards down the road, both feet on the brake and sparks flying all over the place from the Chevy fender he was dragging behind him. It took almost another hundred yards to get the Torino under control and brought to a complete stop. With his hands shaking and his heart pounding, Jennings looked into his rearview mirror. A single headlight sat motionless in the center of the highway far behind him. The sheriff's fear slowly began to turn to a sense of rage. In his present state of mind, Jen-

nings concluded that Walker had just tried to kill him.
Now he had his ass. Attempted murder of a peace officer . . . yeah, that's what it was. Now he could say it was
justifiable homicide.

Releasing the .357 magnum from his holster, Jennings
swung the Ford around in the road and started back
toward the Chevy. Once the car was in his headlights, he
eased the Torino slowly forward. Steam rose from the
front of Walker Kincade's car. When the fender had been
ripped off, some of the bolts had been thrown forward
into the fan and perforated the radiator.

Walker had thought of trying to run the Chevy until
the engine blev, but what was the use. The shattered
ankle and loss of blood from the leg wound had finally
become more than he could bear. As far as he was concerned, it was over. Placing his hands at the top of the
steering wheel, Walker lowered his head to rest on his
arms—he was so tired.

Jennings sat in his car for a moment and stared at the
Chevy. He could see Walker's hands and head resting on
the steering wheel. Stepping out of the Torino, he walked
to the front of the tripper's car. Seven holes were visible
on the passenger side of the windshield where the double-
odd buckshot had blown out the rear window, passed
through the car and out the front glass. He could only
imagine what it had been like riding in that car with all
that lead flying around.

Jennings yelled, "Get out of the fuckin' car!"

Walker heard him, but didn't move.

Raising the magnum, Jennings yelled again, "I said
get the hell out of that damn car, Kincade, or I swear I'll
shoot you where you sit."

Walker managed to raise his head slightly and stared
out at the sheriff and the big gun in his hand. "You and
your boys done shot the hell out of me, Jennings. And I

think my ankle's broke, so I think I'll just save myself the fuckin' walk."

For a scant moment Walker thought that Jennings might actually arrest him, but as their eyes met, he saw that was nothing more than wishful thinking. As the sheriff's face took on a wicked grin, his thumb went to the hammer of the .357 magnum and began to ease the hammer back slowly.

Walker took his hands from the wheel and leaned back in the seat. He thought of his wife and the baby that he knew he would never see. Jennings was saying something. Walker could see his lips moving, but he couldn't hear a word the man was saying. The loss of blood was having its effect. He was wavering on the verge of passing out. Even the pain in his ankle had lost any meaning. In a strange way he wished Jennings would just get it over with. Yet, deep down, he still retained the Kincade trait of never giving up no matter what the odds or the situation.

"Hey, Walker," yelled the sheriff, "you got any last request before I send your ass to bootlegger hell?"

Maybe it was the way the lawman said it, or the stupid grin he had on his face, Walker wasn't sure, but for whatever reason he felt the sudden surge of determination rise within him. A determination to live or at least take the fat son of a bitch with him. Raising a hand slowly to his shirt pocket, Walker pulled out a pack of cigarettes. "How 'bout one last smoke, Jennings?"

Lowering his gun, Jennings was laughing at his own joke as he said, "Sure, boy! But ya know they say them things can kill ya!"

Walker forced a smile and pulled out a single cigarette allowing the lawman to see his hand shaking.

"Scared shitless, ain't you boy?"

Fumbling with his lighter, Walker tried to make it

sound like he was on the verge of tears as he replied, "Yes, sir. I surely am."

Finally lighting the cigarette, Walker intentionally burnt his finger, dropping the cigarette, "God damn it!" exclaimed Walker, "You got me so shook I can't even light a damn smoke."

Jennings was loving every minute of this. He had the great Walker Kincade cowering before him like some sniveling street punk. He was so full of himself that he never gave it a second thought when Walker leaned down to retrieve the lit cigarette.

Reaching for the cigarette, Walker's hand came back to the front of the seat, his thumb triggering the release on the mounted .45. The gun slipped smoothly into his hand. He placed it in his lap and brought the cigarette up to his mouth.

Jennings had to admit, Walker Kincade was one cool character. A series of flashing lights suddenly appeared down the road. His deputies were coming. "Time's up, Walker. Gotta have you dead before the boys get here. Clear-cut case of resisting arrest, you see."

Jennings brought the magnum up again. Walker surprised his adversary with a wide grin, then he shouted, "Wouldn't want you havin' to lie to the law, Jennings— so I guess I better resist."

In the split second it took Jennings to figure out what Walker had said, he was dumbfounded to find himself staring down the barrel of a Colt .45 automatic.

Both men fired at the same instant. The magnum tore through Walker's right shoulder with devastating effect. At the same moment Jennings clutched his side as he was knocked back by the impact of Walker's .45 slug that tore through his body.

Walker's body shook and the pain was unbelievable. Reaching across with his left hand, he pulled the dump release. One hundred gallons of pure moonshine spilled out onto the highway. Grabbing the door handle, Walker managed to throw himself out of the car, landing with a jolt on the grass beside the road. He was dazed and confused and there was a strong smell of alcohol mixed with gasoline. Where was Jennings? He'd seen him go down, but where was he?

The answer came in the form of a loud roar as the magnum fired and a .357 slug plowed up the dirt only inches from Walker's head. A second slug ripped through Walker's leg, shattering the right kneecap. The traumatic shock of the wound was more than Walker's body could stand. He was going to die—he knew that now. As a hazy darkness began to close in around him, his eyes cleared long enough for him to see Jennings on his knees in front of the Chevy. He was struggling to raise the magnum for a final kill shot. The deputies arrived. Bringing their squad cars to a screaming halt, they jumped out with their weapons, trying to assess the situation.

Walker could feel his life's blood leaving him. Nearly blind and with only enough strength remaining to raise the .45 a few inches, he pulled the trigger with his dying breath.

The bullet was nowhere close to hitting Jennings, but it struck the pavement near the front of the Chevy. The deputies had started to cross the highway, but the sparks from that single bullet were enough to ignite the highly volatile mix of alcohol and gasoline. In a split second a huge fireball erupted that lit up the Carolina night sky. Sheriff Bill Jennings was in the middle of that fireball. His inhuman screams came out of the flames. The deputies raced for the fire extinguishers in their squad cars, but it was too late to do any good. As they attempted to approach the burning body, the flames spread to the Chevy gas tank and exploded, sending them scrambling for cover across the highway. As the flames died down, one of the deputies called for an ambulance while the others put out the fire.

With nothing to do but wait, the three deputies stood silently surveying the senseless death and destruction that lay all around them. "You know, Kathy down at the diner just told me the other day that Walker got out of the trippin' business. I didn't really think he'd be on the road tonight."

Another lit a cigarette and exhaled long and slow before he said, "Too bad he didn't. Always thought Walker could have made it on the racing circuit if he'd had a big time sponsor. The boy sure could drive."

The other two nodded in agreement. "Claire is expectin' ain't she?" asked one.

"Yeah," said the smoker. "Gonna' be their first. This'll sure make things tough on her."

"Yeah, but she's got Walker's brothers. You can bet Charlie and Rich will take care of her. Them Kincades are a close family."

The bodies were bagged and moved to the side of the road. As they looked at the sheriff's body one of the deputies said, "Guess it's better it ended this way. If Bill hadn't died tonight, Charlie and Rich would have got him before the week was out. Then we'd had to lock them up and had three families without a daddy."

"Who's gonna' tell Bill's wife?"

"Guess I will," said the senior deputy. "Then I'll have to break the news to his girlfriend, Abby."

"Abby!" said the younger deputy, surprised at hearing the name. "Abby Randall, the daytime dispatcher?"

"Hell, yeah. Ol' Bill's been doin' her on the side ever since he hired her a year ago."

The squad car radio came to life. "1012, this is dispatch. Come in."

"Dispatch, this is 1012. Where the hell's our ambulance?"

The deputy could hear the curiosity in the dispatcher's voice as she asked, "Hey, Carl, you didn't say who this ambulance was for. Anybody we know?"

"We'll talk about it when we get in, Hattie. Now what's the hold-up on the ambulance?"

"They're on another call—Claire Kincade. She's having her baby this morning. If you happen to see Walker out there anywhere you might tell him to get his butt to the hospital. She's been asking for him. God, I hope he ain't out there trippin' again. He promised her he'd give that up. He's not still trippin' is he Carl?"

The deputies stared at each other in silence. Carl glanced over at the burnt-out Chevy, then at the body bags near the road. Pressing the button on his mike, Carl replied, "No, Hattie. Walker Kincade's made his last run."

4

"And Charlie Kincade is makin' his move, folks! With two laps to go, this is gonna' be a pedal-to-the-metal, all out run, so hang on to your seats!"

The crowd was on their feet and they were screaming for all they were worth. It wasn't for Charlie Kincade, but rather for Earl Weaver, a local boy who had been a dirt track champion and favorite for a number of years, that is, until the arrival of the Kincade clan on the dirt track circuit.

Now in their early fifties, Charlie and Richard Kincade had given up the moonshine business for good after the death of young Walker. Some said it was out of respect for their brother. Others said it was because Walker's death had scared the hell out of them, but anyone who really knew the Kincade boys knew that nothing

that walked, crawled, or flew could scare those two boys.
The truth was that after Walker's death, they not only had
responsibility for their own families, but for the care and
welfare of Claire and her newborn son as well.

Both had done prison time for running in the early
days. A second conviction and they knew they'd be put
away for a long time. By the seventies, the risk just didn't
measure up to the shrinking money from a business that
was quickly vanishing from the American scene. There
were still quite a few stills producing up in the hills, but
it was more for local consumption than anything else.
Oh, there was still the occasional big-money load
required for a special event or get-togethers, but those
were few and far between. Nothing a man could support
a family on, that was for damn sure.

No, the Kincade brothers needed respectable jobs with
stable incomes. It was only natural that those jobs would
have to involve engines and cars. There wasn't a better
mechanic to be had anywhere than a former tripper, and
the big-name dealerships were quick to recognize that
fact. All a former runner had to do to guarantee himself a
job with one of those dealerships was to write the word,
"tripper" in the space allocated for former occupations.

One week after burying Walker, the brothers had gone
to Charlotte and gotten themselves steady jobs with the
largest Ford dealership in the area. They had hoped to
find work closer to home; Charlotte was a ninety-minute
drive one way. The closest town of any size that could
afford to pay them the kind of money they required was
Collinsville, located at the base of the mountain, but they
quickly discovered that the name Kincade was treated
like the plague by the so-called good people of that town.
After all, that was the town where Sheriff Bill Jennings
had been born and raised. He had been one of their own.
And from their version of the story, Walker Kincade had
been guilty of nothing less than outright murder. Murder

of a law enforcement officer. A fine officer, or so they thought, who left behind a wife and two young daughters. Of course, no one mentioned the sudden disappearance of Abby Randall from the department a few weeks later. Nor did it matter that all of the deputies' sworn affidavits emphasized Sheriff Jennings's state of mind at the time or the fact that not one of them could say who fired the first shots that led to the death of both men. The good people of Collinsville had, on their own, assumed that since Walker was a known tripper and a violator of the law, then he must have been the one to instigate and force the tragic events that took Sheriff Jennings's life. And nothing was going to change their minds about that.

Claire had never remarried. Not that she hadn't been asked by a host of suitors over the years. But there had only been one man for her and he had died on the very night their only child had been born. Thankfully, the uncles had been there for her during the hard times. They had never wanted for anything and Charlie and Richard had raised Jack as if he were their own son. It had been a highly emotional time for Claire. The joy of a son, shared with the sadness of losing a husband and father. Then there were the ugly things that were said about Walker over the years. But as hard as it had been for her, it had been twice as hard for young Jack growing up. On more than a few occasions he had come home from school, his face bruised, clothes torn and a bloody lip or nose. All the results of fights he had had with older boys who had taunted him about the father he'd never known. Although he never complained, she would often hear him crying softly in his room.

Claire had watched her son grow tall and strong, each day that passed reminding her of how much he was like his father. The same gentle voice, the same mischievous grin when he was up to something he knew he shouldn't be doing. By the time he was fourteen, his uncles had taught him how to take a car apart and put it back together. They had also taught him a few things about self-defense—something that Claire at first had objected to, but quickly recanted her objections the first time Jack had come home with a busted lip, but with a wide smile on his face as well. That smile told her that Jack had finally stood up to his tormentors and won. From that day on there were few at his school foolhardy enough to mess with Jack Kincade.

Richard and Charlie Kincade had done well for themselves over the years. Rich was now the chief mechanic for the largest Ford dealership in Charlotte, while Charlie had figured if he was going to work on other people's cars, he might as well get all the money for it. Putting all his money together, Charlie had bought himself a garage. It had grown from a small three-stall, cinderblock affair into a major top-of-the-line shop that covered over 20,000 square feet, and he had more work than he could handle. He employed ten full-time mechanics, all former trippers. Charlie guaranteed the work on every car they serviced. The people of Collinsville may not have thought much of the Kincade name, but in the ever-growing populace of big-city Charlotte, it was a name synonymous with quality work and straightforward honesty.

You could take the boys out of the moonshine business, but you couldn't take the love of big engines and fast cars out of the boys. By the late seventies, the brothers had begun racing late-model stock cars on the weekends at dirt tracks all over the South. They had watched the sport grow from a group of good-old-boys racing for side bets to a multi-million dollar spectator sport that now drew national attention.

They had begun racing in 1979 and quickly learned that there was more to track racing than just speed. It was one thing to go ripping down a mountain road at breakneck speed, outrunning anyone or anything chasing you, but a totally different thing when you had to apply that same nerve and speed to an oval track of hard-packed clay and dirt. On a tripper run, you had the entire open road in front of you. Speed was still a necessity, but not any more important than skill and maneuvering. A driver had to know when to punch it and when to back off; when to hang, looking for that one opening or mistake that would allow him to shoot through the gap and put him in the lead. Then once in front, how to hang on to that lead.

That first rookie year had been a disaster for the Kincade brothers. They had taken some hard knocks right along with the two cars they had put together, but they had also learned some valuable lessons about what it took to move up the win chart in dirt-track racing, especially where money was concerned. And now, seven years later, through trial and error, those lessons were paying off. The rise to prominence began in 1982 with four first-place wins at the largest dirt tracks in Atlanta, Charlotte, Macon and Darlington. Over the last four years they had become a holy terror, claiming top victories throughout every major dirt-track competition in the south.

This final race in Macon would be their last of the year and if Charlie could pull it off, they would finish number one in both the money and points standings and lay claim to the Southern dirt-track circuit championship—a goal they had been chasing for seven long years.

For Charlie and Rich, the only thing more important than racing was family. Especially young Jack. They had watched him grow over the years and like Claire, with each year's passing they could see more of their brother Walker. The looks, the walk, the excitement in his voice when he talked about racing as he traveled with them every weekend from track to track.

Charlie had built a half-mile oval dirt track on the land

behind his garage. Once they had put a car back together following a race, they let Jack put it through its paces on that track. That was when they truly felt they were in the presence of Walker's spirit. Jack was a natural, just as his father had been. Natural ability, courage and a love for cars and speed. There was little doubt in their minds that one day Jack would be taking their place behind the wheel and the pole positions on the weekends.

Standing on top of one of the Kincade cars, Jack was waving his arms frantically and cheering Charlie on. Richard watched him for a moment and smiled as he thought, "God, Walker would have been proud of this boy."

"Hey, Uncle Rich," yelled Jack. "Would you believe Weaver's trying to sucker Charlie into a gap on the high side. He must have forgotten who he was runnin' against out there."

Richard climbed up on a fender to watch the first- and second-place cars come out of the turn sideways on the far corner. Out of a field of twenty-four cars, only eleven were left in the race and Charlie and Weaver had already lapped the other nine.

Dirt flew thirty feet into the air as both cars leveled out and accelerated down the straightaway side by side. Weaver had purposely slowed on the turn hoping to sucker Charlie into going up on the high side to pass. He could then move halfway up to the center of the track to keep Charlie pinned high until the final turn, then drop back into the low slot and use the shorter distance to take the flag. It was a good plan, and might have worked on a rookie or a driver with limited experience, but Charlie had been around way too long to fall for that.

The key to Weaver's great plan was to keep Charlie blocked off, or pinned on the high side of the track. The bad part of the plan was assuming that Charlie would allow himself to be cut off and pinned on the high side.

Jack gave a questionable look in Rich's direction as he heard his uncle say, "Oh boy—bad idea, Weaver!" They had started into the third and final turn before the finish line. Just as Weaver began to think that his plan had worked and he had Charlie where he wanted him, Charlie backed off just enough to allow the rear of Weaver's car to come in line with the front of his left fender.

From the infield, Rich and Jack watched intently. The cars were just about to come out of the turn when Rich grinned, then laughed and shouted, "Swing your partner, brother!"

At the same instant, Charlie cut his wheels hard left and the right front of his car clipped the left rear of Weaver's car and sent it spinning around and around until it spun out of control and ended up against the infield wall. In the stands the crowd was on their feet. Half were cheering while the other half were booing and flipping Charlie the finger as he went around on the victory lap.

Jack was jumping up and down so hard he was about to cave in the top of the car. Turning to Rich, he hugged his uncle. "You did it! You took it all! I knew you guys could do it. Wait'll I tell Mom. I been tellin' her this was your year."

Richard held the boy tight as if he were his own son, which in a way he was. Of all the Kincade children, Jack had been the only one to show an interest in cars and racing. Slapping the boy on the back, and with a tear in his eye, Rich said, "No, son, *we* did it! You're just as much a part of this team as me and Charlie, and don't you forget it."

The Kincade crew's party on the infield had just gotten started when Earl Weaver and six of his crew came pushing their way through the crowd that had surrounded the winners and their car. Jack was the first to see them coming and from the way they were walking and the hard look in their faces, he knew there was going to be trou-

ble. Charlie and Rich were laughing and dancing arm in
arm when Jack moved to their side and said, "Weaver and
some of his boys are comin' this way. And I don't think
it's to give us a kiss and a pat on the ass."

The sounds of celebration quickly began to fade as the
crowd around the brothers separated, allowing Weaver
and his crew to pass. Rich and Charlie glanced at one
another, then smiled as Charlie whispered, "Had an idea
these boys wouldn't be the good-loser type."

"God, I hate when you're right," replied Rich as the
brothers placed their backs against their car to prevent
anyone from coming up behind them. At the last second,
Jack stepped in between his uncles. "Now, Jack, this
might not be a good idea. Your mama'll whip me and
Charlie both if you get hurt," said Richard.

Jack looked his uncle straight in the eye. "You said we
were a team. Well, a team sticks together, on or off the
track." That ended the discussion, but those that had
overheard the boy's answer couldn't help but note the
sense of pride on the faces of the two older men that
flanked the tall, good-looking boy in the middle.

Earl Weaver stood six-foot-two, with burly arms and a
beer gut that hung a good five inches over a gaudy silver
belt buckle half the size of a pie pan. Stopping a few feet
in front of the brothers, he pointed a chubby finger in
Charlie's face. "You mother fucker! You tried to kill my
ass out there. You fuckin' cheated. That's what you done,
God damn you!"

Jack watched Weaver's backers spread out, forming a
semicircle around the Kincades. They were all good-
sized men and appeared as accustomed to brawling as a
preacher giving sermons on Sundays. Jack couldn't help
thinking that they were going to get their asses kicked,
but he wasn't about to let them see any sign of fear on his
face. Picking out the biggest guy there, Jack gave the
man a taunting grin that clearly conveyed a threat.

Three more members of the Kincade team, all mechanics from Charlie's garage, moved to the front of the team car to even up the odds. The crowd began to form a circle around the opposing forces in anticipation of an old-fashioned donnybrook breaking out at any moment. Some in the crowd had already begun taking bets on who would be standing when the fight was over.

From the booth above the grandstands, the race officials saw the crowd gathering on the infield. Bud Taylor, the track owner, lowered his binoculars as he swore, "God damn it! I was afraid this would happen if one of those Kincade boys won."

Turning to his track manager, Taylor barked, "Jake, round up some of the boys and get down there. Any of these fans get hurt in a brawl and I'll have lawsuits comin' outta my ass!"

Jake Dunn hesitated for a moment. He wasn't all that wild about the idea of jumping into the middle of any fight that involved the Kincade brothers. Earlier in the year he'd had a chance to watch Charlie and Rich take on five burly guys in a bar outside Atlanta. In a wild race earlier that night, the brothers had managed to put three cars into the wall. Some said it was by accident, others said it had been on purpose. No matter that the brothers hadn't even placed in the money that night. There were still those that thought they should be taught a lesson. Two things had impressed Jake Dunn that night: one, the Kincade brothers' total disregard for the fact that they were outnumbered by a group of toughs half their age, and second, the speed with which these two older men had dispatched their opponents—leaving all five unconscious, scattered on the floor, bar, and pool table. No, Jake Dunn wasn't all that thrilled about his boss's idea.

"Uh . . . boss, you know . . . I think maybe we should, uh . . . let them boys, you know, work this thing out

among themselves . . . I mean, kinda man to man. I'm
pretty sure they—"

Bud Taylor's face was a crimson red as he turned on
his track manager. "I ain't payin' you to fuckin' think,
Jake. Now get your people down there and break that shit
up—and I mean, now!"

Jake shook his head and moved to the door, mum-
bling, "Ain't my fuckin' track! Why don't you take your
fat ass down there and—"

"What's you say?" barked Taylor.

Jake glanced over his shoulder as he was going out the
door and answered, "Said, I'll get some of the boys and
break that shit up, okay!"

Rounding up every security man he could find, Jake
headed his group across the track toward the ever-growing
crowd on the infield.

The Kincade boys and their crew were waiting
patiently for Weaver to complete his ranting, swearing
and slandering of everything from their dead brother,
Walker, to their wives, mother, and even their dogs. He
especially questioned the legitimacy of their birth, insist-
ing that they were even lower than mere bastards.

Having allowed the overweight loudmouth to express
himself for a full two minutes nonstop, Charlie shot a
glance at Jack and Rich and winked. Looking back at
Weaver, Charlie raised his hand and waved it slowly back
and forth. "Whoa, there Hoss. Hold it right there."

Weaver's face was red as a beet and the veins were
visibly throbbing at the side of his head as he shouted,
"Yeah! What the fuck ya' got to say?"

A hush fell over the crowd gathered around them.
Charlie's voice was low and calm as he asked, "Now, just
what the hell was it you said about my dog?"

Weaver's eyes went blank and his face took on a look
of confusion as if he were trying to understand the question or remember what it was he'd said.

"That's what I thought you said!" shouted Charlie as he swung his left foot up, catching Weaver solid between the legs and lifting the big man a full two feet off the ground. At the same instant, Jack leaped forward and delivered a head-butt to the giant in front of him. The sound of the big man's nose breaking was clearly heard through the crowd. Richard ducked a wild swing and drove an elbow into the midsection, which doubled his attacker over. Taking a half step back, at the same time bringing his knee up as hard as he could, he sent the man flying backwards into the crowd.

Within seconds everyone within a thirty-foot radius was involved in the brawl, which was rapidly spreading into the crowd. By the time Jake and his security men, dressed in black, broke through the crowd, there were more than thirty people going at it and fists were flying. "Okay, boys! Let's get in there and break this shit up!" shouted Jake, who took a couple of steps forward, then, as his security men rushed into the brawl, quickly backed away from the eye of the storm to assure he was out of harm's way.

It took twenty minutes to get everything calmed down and some sense of order restored. The people in the crowd that had put their money on the Kincade brothers went around collecting their winnings. Bud Taylor stepped to the front of the crowd that was still gathered and surveyed the damage. There were close to fifteen people still sprawled out on the ground, either out cold or barely moving. Weaver and his entire crew were among those still out. Four of the security people were down, but beginning to move around, as well as five people from the crowd that had obviously chosen to back the wrong side.

Leaning against their car, the Kincade boys and their crew were passing around a bottle of Jim Beam. Their faces were a bloody mess, but that didn't seem to bother any of them. Jack's shirt had been torn off his back and Rich and Charlie's might as well have been—they were no more than mere rags hanging on the two brothers. Seeing Taylor walking toward them with an envelope in his hand, Charlie took a few steps forward, wiping the blood from his mouth. He smiled and said, "If it's okay with you Mister Taylor, we'll skip the formal bullshit. I'm afraid we're not quite dressed for any fancy ceremonies. We'll just take the money and head to the house before there's any real trouble."

Taylor was furious. "And just what the hell you call this?"

Charlie reached out and took the envelope from the owner's hand. "Oh, this here was just a little misunderstanding about a fellow's dog." With a smile, Charlie walked back to his team. "Let's load'em up and head for the house, boys." Holding the envelope high above his head, he continued, "Breakfast at Denny's on me."

Bud Taylor's temper was at full throttle. Everything he'd planned for the ceremony following the last race of the season was in a shambles. The band from the local college that was supposed to play during the winner's lap and following the trophy presentation were already filing out the gate. The mayor and the three high-level representatives from the stock car association were still standing on the platform at the finish line, surrounding a three-foot silver monstrosity that had had no chance of competing with the all-out brawl that had taken place on the infield. And all of this had taken place before the biggest crowd Taylor had drawn to the track since he had built it ten years ago. To say the man was pissed was a total understatement in any terms, and somebody was going to pay.

Jake Dunn just happened to walk up at that very moment, giving credence to the old saying of "being in the wrong place at the wrong time."

"I think we were damn lucky more people didn't get hurt, huh, boss."

Bud Taylor turned all his anger into a cold glare which he cast at Dunn. "You're fuckin' fired! Now, what'd you think about that?"

Dunn looked down at Earl Weaver who was still on the ground puking his guts up, then at the members of his crew who still littered the ground and were barely moving. Jake shook his head and with a half smile replied, "That just suits me fine, Mister Taylor. At least I can still see outta both eyes, my nose ain't broke, and I can walk without my balls bumpin' my back teeth. But I'd highly suggest that the next time you have them Kincade boys on this track, you bring in the national guard. See ya round, asshole!"

5

The Kincade boys were still celebrating as they headed
down the interstate. "Jesus, did you see the look on that
Weaver's face when you asked about that dog?" said
Rich. "I thought I was gonna' split a gut right there. That
was priceless, Charlie."

Jack was laughing right along with them, but not quite
as loud. His jaw still hurt from a blindside shot he'd
taken during the fight. He hadn't seen who threw it, but
judging from the impact, he figured it was a guy named
Mac, like in a Mack truck.

Charlie glanced over at his nephew. "Hey, Jack. You
done real good out there. Handled yourself pretty, son."

"Course, I wouldn't say anything about that to your
mom," said Rich.

"Yeah," added Charlie. "She'd have me an' Rich out
behind the woodshed for sure."

Jack managed a grin, "You really think so?"

"Oh, yeah. Only two things your ma didn't like your
dad doing. One was trippin' and the other was fightin',"
said Charlie.

Jack thought about that for a second, then asked, "Could Dad handle himself, Charlie?"

"Could he? Let me tell ya' boy. Your ol' man could have took on that whole Weaver bunch all by himself and it woulda' come out the same. He was a real scrapper, your dad, yes, sir."

"I'm surprised your mom hasn't told you about some of his more famous moments, Jack," said Rich. "But then, like we said, she never could tolerate fighting or brawling. She would always tell your dad he was better than that."

Jack sat in silence for a while, trying hard to form a picture in his mind of a father he had never known, but there weren't a lot of pieces to put together. He really didn't know much about the man. His mother had shown him pictures and he could never recall her saying a single bad thing about him. He'd actually learned more from his uncles, but even that had come in bits and pieces over the years, much like the conversation they were having tonight. But they all had one thing in common. None of them had ever talked about the night his father had died. Everything he knew about that night he had learned from the bullies and assholes at school. "Son of a Cop-killer." That was what they had called him. Well, he was almost eighteen now, and it was time someone started explaining a few things. Staring out the side window, Jack quietly asked, "Charlie?"

"Yeah, Jack."

"I got some questions and I think it's time I started finding some answers."

Both uncles glanced over at the boy. "Like what, Jack?"

"Like how you, Rich, and Dad all got in the moonshine business? How dad learned to drive as good as people say? How he come to end up dying on a mountain road with a dead sheriff and a burning car? Those kinds of questions. The kind nobody's wanted to answer all these years." Turning to face his uncles, he finished with, "Those kinds of questions, Charlie."

Charlie watched the lines in the highway fly by for a long minute then nodded his head. "Guess you're right, Jack. It's time we talked about all those things. They're fair questions and you deserve answers."

Rich saw the bright red-and-yellow sign for Denny's coming up over the next hill. "Charlie's right, Jack. Time we all talked a little Kincade family history, but let's wait until after we have breakfast with the boys. Once they're on their way again, we'll hang back and talk a while. Fair enough?"

Jack nodded his head. "Fair enough."

The next two hours were spent eating, drinking coffee, talking about racing and the fight with Weaver. It seemed to Jack the longest two hours of his life. As much as he liked Woody and the crew, he couldn't help but wish they'd just eat and move on out. He had waited seventeen years for this talk with his uncles and now the thing that stood between him and answers was a bottomless coffee pot and a crew of men that seemed determined to drink the damn place dry.

Finally, Woody Clark yawned, and stretching his arms out, said, "Guess we better get on down the road if we're gonna make Charlotte by morning."

Charlie agreed. "Yeah, Woody. You and the boys head on out. We'll catch up with you."

Woody reached for the check, but before he could get it, Rich snatched it up. "Oh no you don't. You save your money for the nights we don't win."

Woody and the crew thanked them for breakfast and headed for the parking lot. Within a few minutes they were on the road again and headed for home. The waitress brought another round of coffee and as she left, Charlie said, "Okay, Jack. What'd you want to know?"

Jack had been waiting a long time for this opportunity. A young man could formulate a lot of questions over seventeen years, and once Jack began, they came like a rapid-fire machine gun. "Why'd Dad start trippin'? Who taught him to drive? Was he ever caught? What really happened on that road that night?"

Charlie quickly raised his hands. "Wooo, Jack. You're comin' on pretty fast and furious there. Ya' gotta remember, I'm over fifty—I can't even think that damn fast."

Jack grinned then sat back in the booth. "Sorry, Charlie. Guess I just kind of got carried away for a minute."

Rich set his coffee down as he said, "I'll tell you what, Jack. Why don't I start off with a little family history. I think that might answer a lot of your questions, or least cut 'em down considerable. You still got questions afterward, we'll go from there. That be okay?"

Jack agreed. "Sounds like a good idea to me."

Rich took another sip of his coffee, then began. "Well, let's start with your grandpa—our dad. Hardest damn workin' man you'd ever wanta' meet. Wouldn't take a thing he hadn't worked for. That's just how he was. Charlie and me came along in the middle of the Great Depression. Times were hard then, Jack. You young folks got no idea how hard. But your grandpa was just as hard as the times. Then one day he got lucky. He got a job at one of the few mills still in operation outside Collinsville. He worked six days a week, ten hours a day for eighteen dollars a week, and was damn glad to have the job. Your dad came along in 1939. Things were getting a little better by then, but not by much. But you know I can't recall a time that we didn't have fine shoes on our feet and a meal on the table. Pa kept making the trip five miles down the mountain to work and five miles back every night. He had to walk it, Jack. We didn't have no car or truck back then. That hard old man made that trip six days a week, fifty-two weeks a year and never missed a day. Didn't matter, scorching heat or freezing cold, he was always there."

Rich paused a moment, his eyes staring out the window as if he could somehow see his father making that long walk in the dead of winter. He'd never heard that old man complain, never once in all those years. It was clear to Jack where the Kincade family got its toughness.

"The war came along—December of forty-one," continued Rich. "Pop tried to join up, but his knees were shot. All those trips up and down that mountain I guess. But, in a way it was for the best. He got a promotion to foreman at the mill and a hefty raise along with it. Six months later we got our first car. A 1939 Ford Coupe. Pop never had to walk that mountain again.

"By the end of the war, Charlie was sixteen and I was fifteen. Between school and taking care of Ma's garden, we started tinkering with that old Ford Coupe. Pop had got a truck by then and told us we could have the Coupe. Within a year we learned to take that car apart and put it back together over a weekend. Walker was only seven years old then, but anytime we were messing with that car, he was right there, and always asking questions.

"Pop got another raise at the mill the following year, and we figured he'd get another truck and we'd get the old one, but then one day he came up to us while we were working on the old Coupe. He asked if we'd been racing the Ford for money. Of course we had been racing it against a bunch of the local boys outside Collinsville, but we lied and told him no. What we didn't know was that part of the money we'd won that weekend came from the kids of a couple guys that worked for him at the mill. He didn't say another word. Just stared at us for a long time, then walked off.

"The next day we came home from school and the Coupe was gone. He'd sold it and gave part of the money to the two guys at work. You see Jack, your grandpa was what they call a righteous man. I never heard him swear, he didn't drink, smoke, lie or cheat. To him the most worthless person in the world was a man that broke the law or gambled. It meant they were too lazy to work like decent people, instead always looking for that easy way at the expense of others. And Lord, how he hated the moonshiners. He'd see them driving their big fancy cars and wearing their fancy clothes and remind us that they were the rewards of evil. He considered them worse than lazy no-accounts that sold misery in a bottle and who profited from that misery. He warned us constantly to stay away from that kind of business. It could only lead to trouble and prison. And I'll be damned if he wasn't right.

"Then one morning, Mama came into our room and told us that Pa was dead. He'd had a heart attack during the night and died in his sleep. That was the winter of fifty-four wasn't it?"

Charlie only nodded, his eyes clearly showing the pain of the memory. Rich went on to tell how it had fallen to twenty-year-old Charlie to take care of the family. He and Rich both had found jobs at a couple of garages outside Collinsville, but the pay wasn't that great and the hours were long. Then one night, Charlie ran into an old buddy. The man had money and was driving a brand-new 1954 Ford. By the time the evening was over, Charlie had a new job. Not as a mechanic, but as a tripper, running illegal moonshine. He was twenty.

Within a year, Charlie had made enough money to pay off the family home. Jack's father, Walker, was fifteen by this time and could already tear down a car and put it back together faster than his brothers ever could. Not only was he a great mechanic, but they soon discovered that he was a natural at handling a car and he loved speed. By seventeen he was lying about his age and running the dirt-track circuit and his room was quickly filling up with trophies. All in all, things were going well for the Kincade clan.

It all came to an end for Charlie in the summer of 1957. He was hauling a load to Atlanta one night when he was trapped and captured by Federal agents outside Atlanta. He was found guilty and sentenced to fifteen years in a federal prison. It was Richard who was expected to pick up the slack for his older brother and assume the responsibility for the family and the home. But Richard's luck was no better than Charlie's. Within eighteen months, Rich was caught hauling a load outside Greensboro and had been sentenced to three years in a state prison by a more liberal judge than the one that Charlie had faced.

This left only eighteen-year-old Walker to take care of their mother and the home. With two boys already serving time, Mother Kincade did everything possible to keep young Walker away from the elements that had put his brothers in prison, but the lure of big money and fast cars proved too much for Walker to resist. By the time he was nineteen, he was running three loads a week and driving the Feds nuts with his ability to evade their road blocks and elude every trap they set for the highly talented driver.

Through good behavior, both Rich and Charlie were soon out of prison. In their absence, young Walker had made a name for himself as one of the hottest drivers to come out of the Blue Ridge Mountains in years. The older boys soon found themselves taking a back seat to their famous baby brother. They both still made an occasional run, but due to the fact that getting caught a second time meant a mandatory sentence of thirty-five years with no parole, they restricted their activities to less dangerous areas of the operation and left the big money loads for Walker.

By the mid-sixties, Walker divided his time between

tripping and racing on the weekends at a number of dirt tracks that had spread across the state. It was during one of those racing weekends that he had met Claire. It had been love at first sight. Six months later they were married and Claire became a welcome part of the Kincade family on the mountain.

Although she never cared for the way Walker made his money, she never complained. It wasn't until she became pregnant with Jack that she began to worry. In the months before his death, they had argued a number of times about his line of work, Claire all the time stressing the importance of responsibility for a new father.

Richard paused at this point of his story and stared silently into the coffee cup in front of him. Jack saw the signs of tears welling up in his uncle's eyes and respectfully remained silent. Charlie seemed to be equally affected by the moment. Jack's mother had been right. The memories of their brother and the tragic events that had led up to that night were still very much alive and painful to these two tough men.

Jack suddenly found himself wishing he had never brought the subject up to start with. These were the two men that had raised him and now it hurt him that he had been the cause of this needless pain. It was an awkward moment and Jack wasn't sure what to say or do to put an end to it all.

Without making eye contact with either man, Jack quietly said, "That's all right, Rich. We don't need to talk about it anymore. I'm sorry I brought it up."

"Nope, you're wrong there, Jack. You got every right to know about your father—how he lived and how . . . how he died. Ain't nobody got more right than a man's son."

"Charlie's right, kid," said Rich, looking up from his coffee cup. "Your dad could've been anything he wanted to be. But you got to remember, we were just mountain boys that grew up in a hard time and a different world than most folks. Fast cars, guns, and bootleg whiskey were all we knew. Hell, they make a big deal out of these stock car boys and their association, but I'll tell you this. Your dad could have left them fellows standin' in the dust any day of the week—he was that good."

Charlie silently nodded in agreement.

Jack was quiet for a moment, thinking of how to ask his next question. But there was no simple or easy way to do it.

"If Dad was so good, why'd he have to kill that sheriff from Collinsville?"

For the first time that night, Jack saw sudden anger building in Rich's face. His uncle leaned across the table and pointed his finger in Jack's face. "You didn't hear that shit from anybody on the mountain! That kind of crap only comes from those sanctified bastards in Collinsville. Your daddy was fightin' for his life that night and it was that son of a bitch with the badge that brought it on himself."

Rich's face had gone red and the still-pointing finger was clearly shaking uncontrollably. "That bastard had been after your daddy for years, but Walker made a fool out of him every time he turned around."

Charlie could see his brother was about to lose it. Reaching out, he slowly pushed Rich's hand down as he said, "That's right, Jack. This fellow Jennings had become the butt of a lot of town jokes because of it. Townspeople began tellin' him he had a better chance of catchin' one of those UFO things, than catchin' Walker Kincade. But it wasn't just the jokes. The town council was on his ass about all the cars that were bein' wrecked, and all the replacements, damages and repairs—hell, it was costin' them a fortune and drivin' the town damn near bankrupt. Some folks say he was about to lose his job over it all."

Rich had began to relax. Natural color returned to his face as he leaned back in the booth. "People figure it all got to be too much for Jennings. He felt your daddy had humiliated him to the point that nothing else mattered but taking him down. He got real determined, kinda' like an old snapping turtle—you know how they can do at times. They latch on to something and they won't let go—hell, you can cut their heads off and they'll keep hangin' on."

Jack shook his head, "So you're saying this got to be a personal thing with Jennings."

"Real personal," said Charlie. "We talked to a deputy that was there that night. He said that the sheriff went clean out of his mind. He didn't want to arrest your daddy. He wanted him dead and that's the order he gave those deputies with him. He didn't want Walter Kincade coming off that mountain alive that night."

"But, God, Charlie! This guy was the law," said Jack, slumping back against the booth.

"No, Jack," said Rich, shaking his head slowly from side to side, "he was a man with a badge obsessed with ridding himself of what he considered the cause of all his problems. He'd convinced himself that he'd lost the respect of the town and the only way he could get that respect back was by putting your daddy in the morgue."

Jack toyed with the handle of his coffee cup as he said, "They say Dad shot him."

Charlie was staring out the window. Without looking at Jack, he answered, "The deputies said there'd been a lot of shootin' at the roadblock. Walker was hit, but he managed to get wheeled around and out of there. Jennings went ballistic when that happened. He jumped into a brand new Ford Torino he'd stole from a dealer and that started a hell of a chase. There was some high-speed bumpin', then a collision and it all somehow ended up in a damn gunfight. Nobody's sure who fired the first shot or why. The deputies got there about the same time the shootin' started. They saw your dad fall out of his car on the driver's side. Jennings must have been hit by then, cause they said he was on his knees in front of Walker's car, firing away with a damn magnum. Your dad fired once from the ground. They saw the bullet hit the pavement. Next thing they knew, Jennings was engulfed in a huge fireball. They figured he was kneelin' in a pool of alcohol and gas that must have leaked from your daddy's car.

"The deputies tried to get to Walker, but before they could cross the highway, the fire spread under his car to the tank and the whole thing went up. The fire . . . covered your dad as well. There wasn't anything they could do."

Jack sat with his eyes closed, his mind having suddenly envisioned that terrible moment. "Was . . . was Dad . . . dead when the car exploded?"

Charlie was on the verge of tears as he glanced over at the young man. "Yeah, Jack. They're pretty sure he was gone before the car blew. He'd been shot up pretty bad before that."

"Good," uttered Jack quietly. "Can't think of nothing worse than burning to death."

The three sat in silence for a long time, each with his own thoughts. Thoughts that were suddenly interrupted by a young waitress wanting to know if they wanted more coffee.

"No, thanks," said Jack. "We were just leaving."

They paid the check and went out to the truck. Before they got in, Jack said, "I know this wasn't easy for either one of you. But growing up, I always had this sense of something missing, kind of like blank spots in my life, you know. I figured it was time I filled in those blanks. I'm really sorry, but I knew there was a lot I hadn't been told and Mom will only talk about the good times . . . now, I know why."

Reaching out, he pulled his uncles to him and they all three hugged. "We all miss him, Jack. Always have," said Richard, trying hard not to cry.

"You ready to head home?" asked Charlie, "Or ya got more questions?"

"No, no more questions, Charlie. And, yeah, I'm ready. The first thing I'm going to do when we get there is give Mom the biggest hug she's ever got from her son."

6

With the racing season at an end, Jack spent most of his time working at Charlie's garage. Business was booming as usual and Charlie, Rich, and Jack divided their schedules between working on customers' cars and the two new cars they were putting together for next season's racing circuit.

Bud Taylor had sent the winner's trophy from the Macon race to Charlie—C.O.D., of course. Along with it came a halfhearted letter of congratulations and a reminder that next season's finals would be held, thankfully, in Charlotte and not Macon. A fact for which he was most grateful; he didn't really think he could afford having the Kincades at his track two years in a row.

The three-foot silver and bronze trophy fit well in the front lobby showcase, where it was surrounded by twenty-one smaller, but impressive, awards that had been won over the last six years. Jack thought it was amusing how Charlie would go on about "those stupid little pieces of tin and metal," but no one could mistake the pride in his face when the customers in the waiting area would ask about them, especially the big one in the middle. He'd personally take them along the line, explaining where each and every one had been won. Although he'd never admit it, the Macon trophy was his pride and joy.

Charlie and Rich had been working on a couple of cars for the late-model stock series. Richard preferred a 1982 Ford T-bird with a 358 engine. Charlie was a Chevy man who also liked the 358 V-8. That was the engine he put into a rebuilt 1980 Monte Carlo. Unlike the cars the big boys ran at Daytona that projected a veiled illusion of being production Fords or Chevys, dirt-track cars were the real thing; lightweight cars with one-carburetor V-8 engines that produced 500 horsepower compared to the 700 horsepower of the big money boys. And big money was the name of the game.

That was something a dirt-track racer didn't have to worry about—he'd never get rich running the dirt circuit, but he damn sure could go broke in a hurry just trying to survive the sport. It was nothing to have twenty to twenty-five thousand dollars in a single car. And if you had to have an enclosed car hauler, you were looking at another twenty thousand dollars.

No, there wasn't a lot of money in it. If a fellow won often enough throughout the year, and could stay out of the wall or escape most of the major crashes, he might—just might—break even, and that would be considered a good year. Yet, every year all across the country, especially in the South, regular fellows finished their day jobs and went home at night to spend another six to eight hours in the backyard or makeshift garage, working on a stock car for the upcoming weekend race at a local track. For the younger guys, it was to gain experience in order to chase a dream that they hoped one day would put them on a track with men like Dale Earnhardt and Richard Petty. For the older guys, who at one time had held that same dream, but had somehow allowed time to pass them by, it was a way to revisit that dream.

Charlie and Richard fit into that mold. They realized early on that they couldn't hold a candle to their younger brother, but they were still pretty damn good drivers in their own right. True, they both knew they were far too old to even think of places like Daytona. Time had gotten to them as well, but the dirt track provided them with the opportunity to envision what might have been.

That Saturday, the brothers were ready to put their cars through their paces on the 3/8-mile track behind Charlie's garage. Howie Price, one of the mechanics, had spent all morning circling the track with a water tanker, wetting it down until it was nearly a muddy mess, then bringing out a heavier truck to pack the mud down until it was almost a slate of pure clay.

Richard was going to make the first run. Cranking up the white-over-blue T-bird, he eased the car onto the track and set a leisurely pace on the first round, getting a feel for the car and the track, at the same time keeping an eye on the gauges for any sign of a problem.

He picked up the pace on the second round. Going high into the second bank, he punched the Ford and shot out of the curve with a roar. By the third time he'd passed the gate he was running at full throttle, taking the curves sideways, whipping out of the slide and ripping down the straightaway. As he tore past Charlie and the boys at the gate, Charlie clicked the stopwatch hanging from the halyard around his neck. Jack kept glancing from the watch to the car fishtailing around the track. Rich was running the Ford wide open, pushing it for everything it had. Flying past the gate again, Charlie stopped the watch. "Not too shabby," he said, showing the time to Jack and the other men around him.

Richard pulled the car off the track near the gate.

Releasing his safety harness, he climbed out of the Ford. "How'd we do?" he asked.

Charlie held the watch up for his brother to see. Rich shook his head. "Damn. I got a lot of vibration on the curves. Must be the suspension. I'll have to run a check on it later today. Otherwise, she feels pretty tight."

Removing the watch from his neck, Charlie handed it over to Richard. "Now that you're through strollin' around the track like some over-the-hill escapee from the rest home, it's time for me to show these boys what a real car can do."

"That's pretty big talk comin' from Mister Senior Citizen himself," said Richard with a grin. The comment brought a chorus of laughter from those around them.

"Senior citizen, huh!" snickered Charlie, as he stepped to the driver side door of the Chevy. "We'll see about that."

Hooking his hands on the top, Charlie started to swing himself up and in through the window, when suddenly he let out a moan. He was stuck half-in and half-out of the car. "Damn, Rich. Get me outta here. I've screwed my back up somehow."

Richard and some of the boys eased Charlie out of the car among a wave of moans and groans. Carrying him to a nearby bench, they carefully set him down. With a look of concern on his face, Jack asked, "You want me to call a doctor, Charlie?"

Charlie shook his head. "Naw, I'll be okay. Rich was right. I keep forgettin' I ain't no damn kid anymore. Got too many years and too many beers hangin' over the belt to be swingin' my big ass through a damn car winda'."

"Yeah," said Rich. "Guess we'll have to start haulin' around a damn A-frame and pulley just to get your ass in the car this season."

Amid the good-natured laughter Charlie replied, "Hey, Rich—screw you, okay. A bad back don't change

the fact that my ol' Chevy can still outrun that damn
Ford any day of the week."

"That a fact," laughed Rich, "An' how you gonna
prove that when you can't even get your butt in the damn
car?"

"I'm not," said Charlie with a sly grin. "Jack's gonna
drive her, and I'll put up a case of Bud that he beats your
time."

The group fell silent as all eyes turned toward Rich,
then to Jack, who stepped forward and said, "Oh, I don't
know Charlie. I don't—"

"I know," said Charlie, cutting him off. "You can do
it. Well, what'd ya' say Mister T-Bird? Is it a bet? Or
have you let that hummin' bird brain of yours overload
that alligator mouth again?"

Even Rich had to laugh at that one before he
answered. "You got it. Go on, Jack. Fire her up, but
don't get too carried away out there. You get yourself
hurt and your ma'll whip all our butts."

Jack's eyes flashed with excitement as he made a mad
dash for the car and practically leaped inside without
touching the frame. Within seconds, he had the big
Monte Carlo moving around the track. While the others
went to the railing to watch the action, Rich sat down
next to his brother. "Okay, Charlie. You can drop the
bullshit. What are you up to?"

Watching the Chevy go up high on the far corner,
Charlie replied, "Just figured it was time we saw what
Jack could do on the track."

"Hell, we both know he can handle the track. He's
done other test runs on cars for us."

"Yeah, but I wanted to give him a little bit of a challenge. See how he handles it, ya know. Figured puttin'
him up against your time might prove interestin'."

"So, you're not really hurt, then?"

Charlie bowed his back slightly as if to prove that he

wasn't, but Rich saw a hint of real pain in his brother's eyes and knew Charlie was lying when he answered, "Naw, I was just fakin' to get the kid to drive. Who knows, we might need him this season."

A worried look came over Rich's face. Charlie could be as stubborn as a mule sometimes. He was in his mid-fifties now and this wasn't the first time he'd had a problem with sudden, unexplained pain deep down in his back, but he flat refused to see a doctor about the problem. Richard was sure there was more to it than just age, but getting Charlie to believe that would take nothing short of an act of God.

Charlie got to his feet. "Awh, quit frettin' like some ol' woman and let's go see if we taught that boy anything."

Jack was still cruising around the track. Swerving from side to side to heat up the tires and get a feel for the suspension, at the same time running high then low, searching for the right groove. Howie Price had a stopwatch in his hand. As Jack came down the straightaway, Howie held up three fingers. Jack nodded that he understood the signal, then began to pick up speed. The three fingers signified that Jack had one lap to get up to speed and that each lap after that would be on the clock.

Coming out of the second turn on the first lap, dirt and clay rooster-tailed behind the Chevy as Jack punched her and kept gaining momentum. As he came out of the last turn and roared past the observers, Howie started the watch.

"Easy, son, easy," whispered Richard as Jack went too high on the first curve, almost losing it. But he quickly regained control and dropped into the slot, flooring the 358 for all she had to make up for the mistake. He came around the second and third turns without a problem. As Jack shot past them at the gate, Howie stopped his watch. At the same instant Rich started his watch to time the second lap.

"How'd he do?" asked Charlie, leaning forward to look at the time.

"Sixteen-thirty four," said Howie. "Not bad, but that slip at the top of number one hurt him on the clock."

"He'll do better on this one," said Rich.

"Damn right he will. He's got his daddy's love for it," said Charlie.

Jack shot through the first turn, dropped to the middle of the track until he found the groove, then punched the Chevy for all she was worth.

"He's goin' too fast for the far corner," shouted Howie. "He'll never make the turn at that speed—he's gotta back off."

"Like hell," muttered Charlie, who suddenly caught himself saying, "Go for it, Walke—I mean, Jack." Rich glanced at his brother. "Kinda' reminds you of his ol' man, don't it?"

With the wind blowing in his face, Jack knew he was coming into the second turn way too fast. Yet, something kept telling him he could make it. He could feel it in the steering wheel, as if the car itself was letting him know that they were both up to the challenge.

As he went into the turn he felt the Big Chevy hold the groove and slingshot him out onto the straightaway with a burst of speed even he hadn't expected. Suddenly, the third curve was there, then gone, leaving nothing but the final stretch that was the straightaway. The crowd at the gate was nothing more than a blur as he shot past them at over ninety-five miles per hour.

"Hot damn!" shouted Rich, staring at the watch. "Fifteen flat!"

Backing off the throttle, Jack cruised around the track, amazed at how natural the last lap had been for him. He knew he had broken nearly every rule of speed and gravity. But it had all happened so fast he was having a hard time figuring how he had done it. Stopping at the gate and crawling out of the car, he was greeted with cheers and slaps on the back by everyone there. "Hell of a run, Jack." "Good goin', kid."

When he looked at his uncles he saw big smiles on both faces. Rich was holding the watch up, showing him the time as he said, "One hell of a show, Jack. You nailed it at fifteen flat."

Jack was actually surprised at the time. He could only say, "Guess that's pretty fast, huh."

That understatement brought a laugh from the mechanics and another round of back slapping before they moved onto the track to take care of the cars.

"Guess I cost you a case of beer, Uncle Rich," said Jack.

"Son, I'm tempted to buy him a damn truckload after watchin' you make that run. You done good, boy."

Charlie gave Jack a stern look. "Ya know you went into that second turn too damn fast, don't ya?"

Jack's head dropped and he stared at the ground as he replied, "Yes, sir."

"Hell, if ya knew that, why didn't ya back it off?"

"Well, sir . . . I . . . I don't know. It was kind of crazy. It was like something in that car told me we could make it. I mean, like if I wanted it to make the turn, then it would. Kind of nuts, huh?"

The brothers each cast knowing glances at one another, before Charlie put his arm around Jack and said, "Not at all son. We knew a young fellow once that could will a car to do just about anything he wanted—your daddy. And I swear, you're a natural just like him."

It hadn't taken long for word to spread about Jack's run. By late that evening practically every mechanic involved with racing from the other garages had heard about it. What Jack didn't realize was that it wasn't just the speed or the time, but the fact that the time had been set by Walker Kincade's son. A fact that seemed to make a number of the local dirt-track boys more than a little nervous. After all, there was that old saying: The apple doesn't fall far from the tree.

It was late and everyone had gone home except for Jack and Howie, who were finishing up a brake job on a customer's car. As they were just finishing, Jack asked, "Howie, did you know my dad?"

"Jesus Jack, I'm only ten years older than you. But I do remember him and my dad working on cars in our back yard. He used to always bring candy along for all the kids. And played with us sometimes, too. I heard my dad say he was the best driver he ever saw. You know, I only saw my old man cry twice in my life. Once, when they notified us that my brother, Neal, had been killed in Vietnam, and the second time, the day he found out your dad had died."

"I'm sorry, Howie. Didn't mean to bring up bad memories."

"That's all right, Jack. Hell, that damn war was a living nightmare for the whole country. Guess it still is for some. I'll tell you something else. My dad said that if Walker Kincade would have had the cash and the sponsors, he could have gave David Pearson and Rich Petty a run for their money on the big show circuit in 1969. He was that good."

That old familiar feeling of emptiness began to creep in on Jack once more. It seemed as though everyone but him had known his father. All Jack had were the pictures and the stories of others to fill that void in his life, and at times—like the run this morning—those things were not enough.

Howie could see the sudden change that had come over the boy. "Ya know, your dad would have been damn proud of that show you put on out there today. Hearin' your uncles talk, I ain't so sure he could've done it any better."

Jack tossed his tools in his tool chest. "Oh, yeah. But that was just running around a damn dirt track. I sometimes wonder how it was for him—trippin', I mean. Knowing that you're hauling a load of illegal whiskey down a mountain road. Knowing that somewhere along that dark highway the feds or the law could be waiting to chase you down or take a shot at you. God, Howie, can you imagine how that must feel?"

Howie paused for a moment, staring at Jack for what seemed a long time, before he answered, "Yes, I can. I know exactly how it feels."

This wasn't the answer Jack had expected. "What'd you mean Howie? How would you know?"

Even though he knew they were alone in the garage, Howie glanced nervously around the building, making certain. "You got to promise me you'll keep this to yourself, Jack."

Intrigued, Jack nodded, "You know I will, Howie. Now what are you trying to say?"

Howie went on to tell Jack how he and a small group of the boys from up on the mountain still made a few runs off and on every year. Mostly for special events that draw big crowds. Everybody, including the feds, thought Big Daddy Wilkes's business had folded up when the moonshine king had died. But that wasn't actually the case. Everything was still in place and now run by Big Daddy's son, David, a hot-shot corporate lawyer in Atlanta. Say there was a big event happening somewhere around your town and you wanted to push a little shine on the side. There were people you could contact, who in turn would contact the Wilkes people in Atlanta. A quantity and a price would be set. If you liked the numbers, the stills went to work and the trippers lined up for the run. Depending on how far the run, the driver could pull down anywhere from a thousand to two thousand dollars.

Jack was sitting on the fender of a car taking all of this in, when he asked, "Okay, Howie. But you can buy liquor, even legal shine in some places now. How do they make any money off this illegal stuff?"

Howie smiled. "Simple matter of numbers, Jack. Liquor stores sell in small amounts for a big price. But moon you can sell cheaper because of quantity. The ol' boy at the liquor store sells a fifth of Jim Beam for ten bucks—he sells ten bottles—he makes a hundred bucks, minus expenses. Wilkes sells a half-gallon of pure mountain blue flame moon for ten bucks, but sells a hundred gallons. That's two thousand dollars. The law of supply and demand, you see."

Jack shook his head. "Well, I'll be damned. I figured those days were long gone."

"They are, really," said Howie. "Like I said, we only get a few runs here and there throughout the year. Like the ones comin' up this weekend."

This bit of news perked Jack up and gained his full attention. "You got a run this weekend?"

Howie lit a smoke before he continued, "Yeah, big Harley-Davidson bikers get-together goin' down outside Winston-Salem. Wouldn't be a real party to them folks without some real mountain dew. Ol' Sparky Thompson figures to make a small fortune off them bikers and they're always more than happy to pay for the good stuff."

"You got that run?" asked Jack.

"Naw, I got a load goin' to Fayetteville. Big special Forces convention goin' on at Fort Bragg. Now them boys really take their drinkin' serious. Long run, but pays two grand. Not bad money for a weekend drive in the country."

There was no disguising the excitement in Jack's

voice as he asked, "Howie, who's making the Winston run?"

Howie thought for a second then replied, "Well, I don't think they got anybody for it yet. I just got the word this mornin' and jumped on the long haul 'fore somebody else could get it."

"Think they'd consider letting me make that one?" asked Jack point-blank.

Howie took a step back like he'd been hit with a two by four. "Wooo . . . Jack! You don't mean that. Man, Charlie would break every bone in my body and Rich'd piss on what was left if I got you involved in this shit. No, sir! I'd just as soon pour gasoline down my drawers and light a match than have them two uncles of yours after my butt."

Jack sprung off the fender and was on his feet as he said, "Come on, Howie. They don't have to know anything about this. Can you imagine how many times I've thought of my dad making a run down that mountain. I've laid in bed at night and wondered what it must have been like. What he thought—how he felt. Why he seemed to love it so much. Now, I'd have a chance to find out for myself."

Howie was shaking his head. "Hell, kid. You can drive down that mountain every night if that's all you want."

"No, it's not the same, Howie. I've done that. Hell, I've been to the exact spot where it all ended that night. It just isn't the same. It's not trippin'."

Howie wasn't saying anything, but Jack had a sense that he was slowly, but surely, winning him over. "Come on, Howie. You know I can drive and you said yourself it wasn't nothing but a weekend drive through the country. Not to mention I could pick up a thousand bucks. What'd you say, Howie?"

Howie dropped his cigarette to the floor and crushed

it out with his boot. His mind was racing. Jack was a damned nice kid. He was Walker's son . . . a thousand bucks, really no risk . . . never knew his dad . . . had a chance to push the clock back . . . be like they were making the run together . . . leave on Friday night, be back on Saturday night.

"Come on, Howie. You can make it happen."

What the hell, thought Howie. If Jack wanted it that bad, who the hell was he to kill the kid's dream?

"Okay Jack. I'll make the call. Tell 'em I got the other driver for the Winston run. Friday afternoon I'll give you the time and directions to the location. You sure you wanta do this? Once I make that call, you're committed."

"More than I ever wanted to do anything, Howie."

Howie knew he'd more than likely live to regret this, but the look on young Jack's face at that moment somehow seemed to make the risk worth it.

Jack stepped forward and grasped Howie's hand. "Thanks, Howie. You're a real pal."

Howie forced a smile. "Well you just remember. Nobody—an I mean *nobody*, can know about this. I mean it, Jack. You say anything to anybody and we'll both be in the shit up to our necks. These boys don't play around."

Jack slapped Howie on the back. "Not to worry, Howie. Seems like I've waited all my life for this chance. I'm not gonna' screw it up now. See you tomorrow."

Jack was humming to himself as he left the garage. Howie went to the main office and picked up the phone. Dialing the number, he waited for someone to pick up on the other end. A familiar voice answered. Just as Howie was about to speak, he felt a sudden chill streak down his spine as he found himself staring at a picture hanging on the wall directly in front of him. There were three young men in their early twenties sitting on the hood of a coal black 1964 Chevy. Charlie on the left. Rich on the right and Walker in the middle. All three seemed to be staring right at him.

"Hello . . . hello. Who the hell is this?"

Howie slowly turned his back to the picture. "Jake, this is Howie. Just wanted to let ya' know—I done got us another driver for the Winston run."

7

It was just past eleven and pitch black when Jack backed off the gas of his 1980 red Trans Am, a gift from his uncles on his seventeenth birthday. The young man's eyes were searching along the shoulder of the highway for the side road he was supposed to take to the loading site. Howie had told him he would mark the spot, but Jack was beginning to get worried. He'd already passed the Hendricks farm a mile back and still there was no sign of a white rag hanging from a tree limb. Maybe he'd missed it. Was it one mile or two past the farm? Should he turn around? Jesus, he was nervous. What the hell was he doing out here anyway? What had he been thinking? He'd already had to lie to his mother, something he'd never done before. He'd told her he was going to Winston-Salem to see a girl he'd met during the racing season. Of course there was no girl, but he *was* going to Winston-Salem.

Jack slowed the Pontiac to a mere crawl as he kept searching the night for the signal. There were so many side roads along this highway that without the rag to identify the proper turn, a guy could spend all night going up and down endless dead-end roads that led nowhere. Frustration began to set in. "Damn it! I've missed it. I know I did." He scolded himself, "Some hot-shot whiskey runner you are, man. Hell, you can't even find the stuff."

Then, suddenly, the strip of white appeared in his headlights. It was as welcome as a flare in the night to a shipwrecked sailor. With a sigh of relief, Jack turned onto the dirt road and disappeared into the dense forest of pines. He began to feel he'd been on the small road forever, but it had actually only been a few minutes. Without warning, a man with a flashlight stepped out from the trees and into the middle of the road. "Jesus!" whispered Jack, as he hit his brakes and brought the Trans Am to a sliding stop.

"Kill them lights!" the man shouted.

Jack quickly did as he was told. He couldn't see a thing. The man kept the flashlight in Jack's face as he moved forward toward the car. Then the man was at the driver's side door and a gruff voice barked, "What's your name, boy?"

"Jack. Jack Kincade. I'm supposed to meet Howie Price out here someplace."

The light clicked off and the gruff voice had lost some of its edge as the man told him, "Well, you done found the right place, sonny. Howie's up that there road 'bout fifty yards or so." The man paused a moment, then asked, "You Walker's boy?"

Jack was still half-blind from the effects of the flashlight, but as his night vision slowly began to focus again he got his first look at the fellow asking all the questions. He was an older man, but big. Mid-sixties, with salt and pepper whiskers and tobacco-stained teeth. He held the flashlight in one hand and a lethal-looking sawed-off shotgun in the other.

"Yes, sir. Walker Kincade was my dad."

"Figured as much. You're the spittin' image of your ol' man. Walkin' up to this car was like lookin' back twenty years. Your daddy was a damn good man, boy. If you got half the spunk he had, you'll do fine." The big man pointed down the road. "They're waitin' for ya' up there. You have good run tonight, ya' hear."

Jack glanced down the dark road for a moment, then turned to thank the man. But just as suddenly as he had appeared from the woods, the old man was gone. Flipping the headlights back on, Jack eased his car forward over the unfamiliar ground. Rounding a bend in the road, the area opened up into what looked like a large campground. He heard the hum of a generator, then spotted it mounted in the bed of a pickup. The generator provided power to a set of lights that surrounded the loading area. Another pick-up held what appeared to be a huge stainless steel tank. The lettering on the side read OWENS MILK PRODUCTS. There were four men standing next to two other cars parked near the milk truck. One of the men was Howie Price, who waved, then came over to Jack's car.

"Yo, boy. Knew you'd make it okay. You sure you still want to do this?"

Jack cut the engine on the Trans Am and for a fleeting second thought of backing out of this whole thing. What the hell had he been thinking? Jesus, this was the same business that had killed his father, cost his uncles time in prison and left his mother a widow with a baby to raise on her own. Yet, knowing all that, here he was anyway.

Howie spoke again. "Well, Jack. What's the call? You in or out?"

Everything about this thing told him to say no. But when he answered Howie, those were not the words that came out of his mouth. "I'm in, Howie. Let's get started."

Howie grinned, "All right, then. Come on, I'll show

you the car you'll be driving tonight. She's a real cherry, man."

The two walked across the open area to one of the cars sitting next to the milk truck. Pointing to what looked like a snow white 1982 Thunderbird, Howie said, "There she is, kid. What'd you think?"

Jack walked around the car once, studying it for a moment, then said, "It looks like an '82 T-Bird, but there's something about it—like it's too short or something. It's not a stocker is it?"

Howie laughed. "Boy, you got a good eye, Jack. She's been put together over a fully fabricated, tubular frame. Shorter in length, and setting on top of a Ford Galaxie-based suspension system. Screw jack-adjustable heavy-duty coils, fully fabricated control arms, twin shocks per wheel, with a sway bar in the front. The rear carries screw jack-adjustable HD coils, panhard rod, trailing arms, Ford nine-inch differential with floating hubs, and twin shocks for both wheels. The brakes are heavy-duty ventilated discs."

Jack shook his head in amazement. "Jesus, Howie. This thing was built for a track."

"That's right." Moving to the front, Howie unlatched the hood and raised it. "An' here's where most of the money went. This is an original three-fifty-one-cubic-inch Cleveland engine capable of puttin' out five hundred horsepower. That'll get you about a hundred and fifty miles per hour on the straightaway. But, Jack, I don't see any need for having to test that theory on this run. You hear what I'm sayin'? The last thing you want to do is draw attention to yourself. But the speed's there if you need it."

Howie closed the hood and moved to the driver's side window. "Your trans is a Borg Warner Super T-10, floor-shift, four speed."

Howie then pointed out a small, black-knobbed lever

located just to the right of the console. "Now that there knob is your drop lever. Once you get to Sparky's garage, he'll have you pull her up onto a phony grease rack. Once he's got you lined up, he'll signal you. You hit that lever and it'll dump the load into his holding tank. That's all there is to it. You get your money and head for the house. It's that simple, Jack."

Jack ran his fingers lightly over the release lever as he said, "And that's it. I mean I just leave."

"You got it, Jack. Pretty easy money, huh?"

"Yeah, Howie, but what about the law?"

Howie laughed, then shook his head. "Not a problem, Jack. This is the eighties. The law don't pay much attention to this kind of business anymore."

Jack still couldn't believe someone would pay him a thousand dollars just to drive this car to Winston-Salem. It was kind of disappointing actually. On the way to the site he'd had visions of high-speed chases, flashing lights, roadblocks and maybe even the crack of a few warning shots being fired. Howie had been right. It didn't sound like any more than a weekend drive through the country. But it was the eighties and the old days were long gone.

"You ready to hit the road, Jack?"

Howie's question brought Jack's thoughts back to the present.

"Ready as I'll ever be."

Howie stepped from the side door of Jack's car. "Okay now, Jack. Just follow me down the mountain. Once we hit the Interstate, I'll be splittin' off and you'll be on your own. You got any questions?"

Jack shook his head. "Nope. I got it."

Howie led the way out to the main road with Jack following close behind. The run down the mountain would take almost an hour. Jack figured it would take longer than that the way Howie was poking along. Hell, he wasn't even breaking the speed limit. They had been cruising at fifty-five since they'd hit the main road and it was starting to get on young Jack's nerves. After all, he had a 351 engine capable of up to five hundred horsepower under him that was just itching to go through the motions. What was the sense of spending a fortune to modify a car for speed if you were going to run the speed limit?

Howie had told him to hang back at least a mile, that way if he ran into any trouble at least Jack would have a good chance of getting away. But every time Jack punched the big T-Bird for a change of pace, he found himself closing in on Howie within a matter of seconds and would have to back off. This was nothing like he had envisioned it. This was the same road his dad and his uncles had run in their heyday as trippers. He'd heard stories of the high-speed chases by revenuers. The wild shooting sprees that had ensued between rival moonshiners and the fiery crashes that had followed. All those things had happened on this very road. The same road where his dad and Sheriff Bill Jennings had had their fatal encounter.

All these thoughts were running through Jack's mind. He could only imagine the excitement and the adrenalin rush of those moments. The more he thought about it, the heavier his foot became on the accelerator. Before he knew it, he was closing in on Howie's taillights again. He started to back off, then thought, "What the hell—I don't need any help getting to the Interstate." The urge to turn the big Ford loose was more than his youthful exuberance could stand. This was more than likely going to be his first and last experience at running illegal liquor. So why not experience it to the max like those that had gone before him?

Dropping down a gear, Jack floored the T-Bird and shot around Howie like he was standing still. The sudden move startled Howie, who muttered, "Damn kid! What the hell does he think he's doin'?"

Jack cranked the window down and felt the full force of the cool night air rushing and whipping through the car. Seventy, seventy-five, eighty. Howie's headlights disappeared from Jack's rearview mirror. At ninety miles an hour, Jack's heart began to pump faster, and he suddenly realized he'd never felt so alive. He'd driven fast before, but this was altogether different. He was amazed at the stability of the car as it hit the curves. He was carrying a hundred gallons of whiskey, yet the suspension balanced out the added weight as if it wasn't even there.

This sense of overconfidence almost cost him on the next curve. He was doing ninety-five when he suddenly felt the rear-end start into a slide, but he quickly recovered. The experience of the moment only served to heighten the excitement as he watched the needle climb to a hundred miles an hour.

Trees, telephone poles and guardrail were nothing more than a blur as the Ford continued to gain speed. Each curve now brought a squeal of tires as they fought to hold the road. The wind, the speed, and the squealing tires projected Jack back eighteen years. He was with his dad now, with Jennings closing in on them at 105 miles an hour. It was all he could do to hold the car on the road. It was both physically and mentally demanding. Jack couldn't imagine having to drive like this after being shot and having a broken ankle as well. For the first time, he realized what a real nightmare that night must have been for his father. The unbelievable pain he must have been experiencing and knowing that he was running for his life.

That single thought had a sudden and sobering effect on Jack. Suddenly, this wasn't fun anymore. The experience had become too real. So real that Jack instantly pulled his foot off the accelerator. He had been doing 120 miles an hour on the straightaway.

The T-Bird backed down to a hundred and was dropping as Jack started into another curve, when out of nowhere his headlights lit up another car parked only a few feet off the side of the road. Jack's eyes were drawn to the symbol on the side of the door. He was moving so fast he couldn't read the lettering, but he didn't have to. It was the seal of the North Carolina Highway Patrol and the man taking a piss beside that car was a North Carolina state trooper.

"Oh, shit!" whispered Jack as his foot automatically went to the brake and he started to slow down. Then it hit him. "What the hell am I doing? I'm carrying a hundred gallons of illegal whiskey and doing nearly a hundred miles an hour and I'm gonna stop? I don't think so!"

Jack figured his only option was to run wide open for the Interstate, which was only five miles away. Maybe—just maybe, he could get there and get lost in the traffic until he could find another exit, then disappear on the back roads. He'd have to do all that before the trooper could zip up and catch up.

Kicking the T-Bird back up to 110, he kept watching the rearview mirror, expecting to see those dreaded dancing red and blue lights at any moment. But they never appeared. Only two more miles to go to the Interstate junction. If he went right on the Interstate he could make the Collinsville exit, then disappear into the town's side streets where he could lay low for a couple of hours until things cooled off.

"Yeah, that's what I'll do," muttered Jack. His heart was still thumping like an overheated Chevy. "God, some big time moonshiner you are! Scared shitless after seeing a cop with his dick in his hand—guess if it'd been a gun you'd have had a damn heart attack!"

The fact that no blue lights ever appeared in his

rearview mirror gave Jack a moment of false hope—hope that quickly evaporated as he topped a hill and saw the Interstate junction flooded in a sea of blue and red flashing lights. So many that it was impossible to count them all. And worse yet, they were all coming straight at Jack.

There was a second of panic, but only a second. With the oncoming swarm of troopers two hundred yards to his front, Jack suddenly hit the brake, cut the wheel hard right, at the same time flooring the T-Bird and executing a perfect bootlegger's one-eighty spin. Where the move came from, he had no idea. He'd heard his uncles talk about it before, but had never attempted the maneuver until that very moment. The fact that it had actually worked startled him more than the fact that he'd even tried it. But even that brief moment of glory was short-lived as he came out of the spin only to find his planned escape back to the mountain blocked by the patrol car he'd surprised along side the road. This time the trooper had something a lot more lethal in his hand—a 357 magnum and it was pointed straight at Jack's head.

Suddenly there were troopers and guns everywhere. Jack was pulled from the car and bent over the hood while the cuffs were locked in place. The trooper he had blown past on the mountain seemed surprised that the driver was so young. "How old are you, boy?" he asked.

"Eighteen next month," replied Jack.

The trooper slowly shook his head back and forth as he said, "Well, Jack, I don't know why you were in such a hurry, but son, you're either suicidal or one hell of a driver. I came down that mountain wide open and never did see those taillights of yours—you must have been flying."

"I was givin' it my best shot," said Jack. "Almost made it too."

The trooper half-grinned. "No, son, I don't think so. They ain't built the car yet that can outrun a radio."

While the trooper was talking with Jack, two other officers opened the doors on the T-Bird and were searching the glove compartment and under the seats for any sign of drugs or weapons, but found nothing. The officer on the passenger side stood up and shouted over the top of the car, "It's clean."

The officer with Jack waved an acknowledgment then asked, "Okay, son. You want to tell me why you were trying to kill yourself coming down that mountain?"

Jack shrugged his shoulders. "Guess I just wanted to see what she'd do and got kinda' carried away."

As Jack was giving his explanation, the officer on the driver side had started to back out of the car when he noticed the unusual-looking lever next to the console. Reaching across the console he ran his fingers over it for a moment as he whispered, "Now what have we here?"

Tightening his hand around the lever, he pushed it forward. Instantly, the overwhelming smell of alcohol engulfed everyone on the scene as a hundred gallons of pure hundred-proof moonshine spread across the highway like a runaway river.

Amid the cussing and warnings being shouted about cigarettes by most of the officers, the trooper talking to Jack looked down at the stream of alcohol running around his shoes, then back at the young man in front of him. "Well I'll be damned, boy. I would have never took you for a tripper. We don't see many of them around anymore—not a lot of profit in it."

Jack nodded in agreement. "Not enough to make it worth all this."

"Well, Jack, for a while there it was just speeding and reckless endangerment. But now, I'm afraid you've graduated to the big time. Running illegal whiskey is still a federal offense. You could be looking at some hard time, son."

Jack's head dropped to his chest. What was his mother

going to think? In that one moment he would have given anything to be back in that clearing in the woods and to have a second chance to tell Howie he'd changed his mind about the whole thing. But all the wishing in the world wasn't going to change anything now. The approach of a blinking yellow light signaled the arrival of the wrecker that had been called to tow the T-Bird away. As the car was being hooked up, Jack was escorted to a patrol car. The trooper opened the rear door for him as he said, "Sorry, son." Jack could see the man meant that.

"I still don't see how you got down that mountain that fast without getting yourself killed."

For the first time that night, a small grin appeared at the corner of his mouth as he replied, "Must have been the extra weight."

Howie eased his Plymouth to the side of the road, a safe distance from the storm of flashing lights. He had arrived just in time to see Jack being placed in the patrol car. Slapping his hand on the steering wheel in frustration, Howie muttered, "Damn it, Jack! Why didn't you stay behind me like I told you to?"

Lighting a smoke, Howie tried to think about what he should do next. He could wait until the area cleared, then continue on with his load. It wasn't his fault Jack had wanted to go hot-doggin' and got himself jammed up. He'd told him what to do, but the kid had screwed it up. Whose fault was that?

That sounded pretty good for a minute or two, but then a sense of guilt began to creep in. All that talk in the garage that night had led up to this and he'd let a boy talk him into putting him behind the wheel, so really, in a way, it was all his fault that Jack was on his way to jail. He should have known the kid was just that—a kid. Hell, he didn't have enough cash on him to go the bail; what was he supposed to do?

Twenty minutes and three cigarettes later, the patrol

cars were all gone and Howie was still trying to figure out a course of action. In the end he knew what he had to do, he just didn't want to think about it. Flipping his cigarette out the window, he turned the Plymouth around and headed back up the mountain to a small restaurant. Digging through the glove compartment he found some change and walked to a pay phone at the corner of the restaurant.

Howie stared at the phone for a long time. God, he hated to do this. He'd worked for Charlie at the garage for over ten years, but he had a gut feeling that wasn't going to matter right now. He thumbed the change in his hand for another minute, trying to think of another way, but there weren't any other options. Dropping the coins in the slot, he uttered, "What the hell, the kid needs help. Maybe ten years will count for something."

Charlie answered the phone. Howie stuttered around at first, but finally told Charlie about the run and how Jack had gotten involved. Charlie never interrupted once as Howie told the story. Finally came the hard part. "Charlie, I'm sorry, but the law got him at the Interstate junction. Wasn't nothin' I could do. They took him away 'bout an hour ago."

There was dead silence on the other end of the line.

"Charlie . . . Charlie, you still there?"

A long pause, then, "Yeah, thanks for callin', Howie."

There hadn't been any cussing or screaming, that had to be a good sign, Howie figured. "Oh, sure Charlie. I'm really sorry. I should've known better than—"

"Howie."

"Yeah, Charlie."

"You're fired."

8

Charlie and Rich arrived at the Haywood County Jail a little past three in the morning. They hoped to post bail and have Jack back home before morning, but that was not to be. The burly desk sergeant with an attitude told them that due to the federal implications, Jack would have to be arraigned by the judge at 10:00 A.M. Until then, the young man would remain a guest of the city. This didn't set well with the uncles, but there was nothing they could do about that. Could they at least see the boy? they asked. The sergeant had to think about that for a moment. The Feds preferred that prisoners that were involved in a federal case not be allowed visitors until after they had interviewed the suspect.

"You the Charlie Kincade that owns Charlie's Garage?" asked the sergeant.

A little surprised by the question, Charlie answered, "Yeah, that's me."

The sergeant's attitude seemed to change, becoming more friendly. "Your boys worked on my sister's car a couple of months ago. Treated her real decent. Gave her a car to drive while they worked on hers. Didn't charge her an arm and a leg and guaranteed their work. Is this boy kin?"

"He's our nephew," said Richard.

The sergeant glanced around the deserted station house before he whispered, "Can't give but maybe fifteen or twenty minutes. Best I can do. That be okay with you?"

Charlie reached across the desk and shook the sergeant's hand. "We appreciate it, Sergeant. Thank you."

Another officer led them downstairs to the cells. Jack was reclining on a bunk in the first cell.

"Twenty minutes, fellows," reminded the officer as he turned and left them alone.

Jack was on his feet. His face clearly showed both the shame and embarrassment he felt at his situation. When he looked at his uncles, he could see the pained expressions at seeing him behind bars.

"What the hell were you thinking, kid?" asked Richard point blank.

Jack shook his head slowly and stared down at the floor. "I . . . I don't know, Uncle Rich. It just seemed like an exciting thing to do at the time. You know, kind of like experiencing the past . . . I don't really know if you'd understand."

"Oh, we understand all right!" barked Charlie. "You got out there a few days ago and made one hell of a run, then figured yourself another damn Junior Johnson or Rich Petty. Figured you was some kind of King of the Bootlegger's or some damn fool thing. Well, let me tell you boy—I knew them fellows when they got started and you ain't no morin' a fart in the wind compared to them boys!"

Jack wouldn't look at Charlie. He'd expected to get an ass-chewing from him, but the words still hurt and he could hear the disappointment in the eldest uncle's voice.

Richard could see that Charlie was so upset that his face was actually turning red. "Okay, Charlie. No sense in making the boy feel any worse than he already does. Why he did it is immaterial now. How we're gonna get him out of this mess is the question."

Jack glanced up at both of them. "Does Mom know?"

"Hell no, she don't!" shouted Charlie, obviously still upset. "An' she ain't gonna know if we can help it. What kind of story did ya give her for bein' gone this weekend?"

Jack's head dropped again as he mumbled, "Told her I was going to Winston-Salem to see a girl I met at a race last season."

Charlie shook his head. "Runnin' whiskey and lyin' to your ma—I don't know which of them makes you a bigger dumb-ass!"

"Charlie! That's enough!" said Richard. "If you're not going to do anything but bitch at the kid, you can haul your butt on out of here and I'll try to figure this out on my own."

Charlie puffed up for a moment as if he were going to bite Rich's head off, then turned away and started pacing the hallway in silence. After a few minutes, he had calmed down and said, "Okay, we've got a kid days away from bein' eighteen. It's his first offense—never been in trouble before this, sole supporter of his mama, and got a steady job . . . what else?"

Neither Rich or Jack could think of anything to add.

"Well, that's it then," continued Charlie. "We'll just have to hope that the judge'll take all them things into consideration. We can put up whatever bond they want an' assume responsibility for him if he'll give him probation. What'd you think, Rich?"

Richard nodded in agreement. As a matter of fact, that sounded pretty damn good. He wondered where Charlie had learned all that and made a mental note to ask him about it someday.

The door opened and the officer that had brought them to the cell said, "Sorry, fellows. Time's up. Sarge says the arraignment's been set for 10:15 this morning in Judge Harting's room. That's on the second floor."

Jack stepped to the bars. "Charlie, Rich. I'm sorry about all this. Guess I wasn't thinking about the consequences."

"Few of us ever do, Jack," said Charlie.

"Not until it's too late," added Rich. "But don't you worry. We'll be in that courtroom with you. And if that judge considers all them points Charlie brought up, then hell, probation would be a winner for us. Come on Charlie, we got to go."

When the door closed behind them, the silence closed in on Jack once again. Sitting on his bunk, he stared long and hard at the bars. He'd only been in the cell for a few hours and already he could feel the small space closing in around him. "God," he wondered, "How could anyone stand being locked behind bars for years?" He'd never really thought much about it before, but Charlie had done three and a half years, and Rich two years, both in federal prisons. The thought of that gave him a new sense of respect for his two uncles. It also helped explain why Charlie had been so upset at seeing him in jail. It was an experience he had hoped Jack would never know.

There were an assortment of people in the courtroom that morning. The lawyers were easy to spot by their five-hundred-dollar suits, three-hundred-dollar shoes, and hundred-dollar ties.

There were three other prisoners on the bench with Jack, with about twenty other people sitting around the courtroom to watch the proceedings. Among them, Jack's uncles. Charlie had managed to locate the lawyer that represented him and his business. He'd arrived at the jail an hour before the hearing and had already talked to Jack, telling him not to worry. Charlie was right. Since it was a first offense he expected nothing more than a possible fine and probation. The lawyer had appeared so confident of that fact that for the first time since he'd been caught, Jack began to feel good about his chances.

The bailiff stood, "All rise," he said. "Hear ye, hear ye. The court of Haywood County, State of North Carolina is now in session. The Honorable Judge William Harting presiding."

Jack eyed the man in the long black robe as he took his place. He guessed him to be in his late forties or early fifties. He had salt-and-pepper hair and piercing dark eyes. Jack knew his fate rested in this man's hands.

The judge and lawyers exchanged polite greetings and the proceedings were under way. Jack's case would be the last of the four that the judge would be hearing this morning. For that, Jack was grateful. There wouldn't be that many people left in the courtroom when the charges were read against him. This whole thing was trying enough without having to be embarrassed in front of an audience.

The first case involved a charge of grand theft auto. Jack thought the prisoner, a man in his mid-twenties, seemed awfully relaxed, almost as if he wasn't even paying attention to the proceedings. Then it became clear— this was the boy's fourth offense in three years. He may not have been interested when it started, but the judge quickly got his attention when he pronounced a sentence of thirty-five years. It took a full five minutes to get the screaming, crying kid out of the courtroom before they could continue.

The next two cases involved the selling of a truckload of hijacked cigarettes and the illegal selling of explosives. The hijacker got ten years and the other fellow, twenty years. As each sentence was pronounced, Jack's confidence began to waver, but his lawyer kept assuring him they would be fine and not to worry. Richard and Charlie had moved from the back of the courtroom to the bench directly behind the lawyer's table.

"Next case," said the judge.

The bailiff rose, but before he could speak, two well-dressed men entered the room and proceeded to the prosecutor's table. Charlie leaned forward and whispered, "Feds."

The two men conferred with the district attorney, all three occasionally glancing over at Jack. One of the men then approached the judge. He had a folder in his hand that he placed in front of the judge. The two conferred for a moment, then the judge opened the folder and began to read the contents.

Leaning forward, Charlie whispered to his lawyer, "What the hell's goin' on?"

The lawyer shrugged his shoulders, "Damned if I know, Charlie."

Jack was getting as nervous as a cat in a room full of mousetraps. After a few minutes the judge nodded to the bailiff to continue.

"Case 1207. The State of North Carolina versus Jack Kincade. The charge is speeding, reckless endangerment, and the illegal transportation of alcohol—i.e. moonshine whiskey."

No sooner had the bailiff finished, than one of the men at the district attorney's table rose. "Your Honor, the federal government also has a number of charges with which they have detailed in the brief before you. We request that the defendant be remanded to the custody of the federal marshal for prosecution by the United States Department of Justice."

Jack had no idea what was going on, but the words federal marshal and Department of Justice didn't sound good. Just what the hell was going on? That was what

Charlie wanted to know. Leaning forward and placing his hand on his lawyer's shoulder, he said, "For what I'm payin' you boy, you better get your butt up there and start talkin'."

Jack's lawyer was quickly on his feet. "We object your honor! This is a state matter, not federal."

The judge settled back in his chair. "Well, now. That's an interesting point of view, Mr. Ripkin. Would you care to enlighten me as to why you are of that opinion?"

Lawyer Ripkin moved forward, pausing in the middle of the room before the judge. "Your Honor. My client was being pursued by a state trooper for speeding and reckless driving. We do not dispute that. However, once he had been stopped and was in the process of being questioned by a trooper, other officers tampered with my client's car, while conducting an illegal search, I might add. It was during this time and only then that the contents of the car were discovered. As I have already stated, as a direct result of an illegal search. Therefore, your honor, I ask that the federal brief before you and the request be denied."

Judge Harting nodded his approval of the way the experienced lawyer had presented his point. But that same point brought a storm of protest from the other side. Soon, the lawyers and the agents were all talking and screaming at each other at the same time, each trying to make his point. "He can't do that! This is clearly a federal case!"

"Like hell it is! Does illegal search ring a bell?"

"The federal court has priority, by God!"

"You don't know what the hell you're talking about!" shouted Lawyer Ripkin.

The sound of the judge's gavel cracked like a rifle shot in the huge room. Instant silence followed.

"Gentlemen, I will not tolerate such behavior in my courtroom. Now sit down, all of you! And shut up!"

No one said another word as the men all returned to their seats. Jack suddenly felt eyes on him. Looking up, he saw the judge staring at him. His heart skipped a beat as Judge Harting said, "Stand up, Mr. Kincade."

Jack was on his feet before he realized it.

"How old are you, son?" asked the Judge.

"Eighteen in July, your honor."

Harting glanced through the file in front of him, then continued, "So you think you want to be a tripper . . . is that correct, Mr. Kincade?"

Jack's mouth was suddenly dry and it was an effort to talk. "Uh . . . no, Your Honor. I mean not a real tripper. I just . . . just thought I'd like to do it once—that's all, Your Honor. Just once."

There was a moment of strained silence, then the judge closed the folder and looked straight at Jack. "Because your father was one of the best trippers in the state. Is that right?"

The question caught Jack off guard. He hadn't been prepared for any mention of his father in this matter. Jack had no idea what to say. Charlie and Rich were equally stunned by the judge's remark.

"He was, you know," continued the judge. "Make a car do things that I didn't think were possible. And those two uncles of yours back there weren't all that bad at it themselves. But you see, they got caught. I'm sure you know what happened to them. Unfortunately, your father wasn't as lucky."

Jack lowered his head, "No, Sir, he wasn't."

One of the federal agents suddenly stood and threw up his hands. "Your honor. I hate to interrupt this little trip down memory lane, but we have a federal case here that I—"

"What's your name, boy!" barked Harting sharply.

The agent appeared a little nervous as he replied, "Jackson, sir. Mark Jackson."

"You're not from around here, are you Mister Jackson?"

"No, your honor. I just transferred here from Boston."

"Well, Sir. You're still not going to be from around here if you don't sit down and shut up. If I decide to open the floor to any motions, you'll be the first to know. Now, sit down!"

Turning his attention back to Jack, Harting asked, "Did the memory of your father have anything to do with you getting involved in this thing, Mr. Kincade?"

Jack looked the judge straight in the eyes. "Yes, Sir. It had every thing to do with it."

Harting shook his head in approval of the straightforward answer. "Well, what do you think I ought to do here, Jack? If I hand you over to Mister Jackson, I'm afraid it could go pretty hard on you. And in case you're wondering, they've got some pretty good points of their own as far as the whiskey business goes."

Jack tried to clear his throat before he answered, but his mouth felt like cotton. "I made the decision to take the run, your honor. Granted, that was a serious error in judgment on my part. But we all have to live by the decisions we make. Right or wrong, I realize that now. Whatever your judgment, I am ready to accept your decision."

Harting was impressed with the young man's statement. Leaning back in his chair, he eyed the three men at the D.A.'s table. He could handle the local boy from the D.A.'s office, but the two federal men were something else. It was apparent that Mr. Jackson was still ruffled by his earlier treatment by the judge. Harting knew his kind. Jackson would love nothing better than to nail this boy to a cross and parade him around as his first big kill in a new area. The problem was, he could do it. They had a number of good legal points in their favor.

He shifted his eyes back to Jack, who was still standing. He'd known this boy's father. Looking at him brought back a flood of memories. He didn't want to see this boy go to jail, let alone a federal prison. Then it came to him—how he could legally keep Jack out of jail and at the same time hold off the federal men. Rocking forward in his chair, he stared straight at Jack.

"Jack, I'm going to give you a choice here. I'm afraid you'll have to make another decision, and this time I hope it'll be the right one. Okay?"

A nervous Jack answered, "Yes, Your Honor."

"Well, then, here's the deal. You can voluntarily join the armed forces. After you have served your tour of duty you may return to this court with proof of an honorable discharge, whereupon all charges shall be dropped and this court will erase all record of this proceeding from your record. Or, you can refuse and I will remand you into the custody of Mr. Jackson's federal marshals. The choice is yours."

Agent Jackson started to protest, but the agent with him grabbed his arm and shook his head. "You don't want to do that," he whispered. "Let it go."

Harting stared at the district attorney's table. He had expected a reaction from Jackson, and was prepared to have him removed from his courtroom if the agent had uttered one word. What he hadn't been prepared for was the wild outburst that came from Charlie Kincade, who was now on his feet and waving a finger at the Judge.

"You can't make this boy join the damn army!" he shouted.

Judge Harting pounded the gavel once. "That'll be enough, Mr. Kincade. Now, sit down and be quiet."

But Charlie was persistent. "The hell I will. This is the U.S. of A. by God, an' that boy's got rights!"

Harting half-grinned as he pounded the gavel again. "Mr. Kincade, you are in contempt of court. That'll cost you five hundred dollars. Sit down."

Richard was pulling at Charlie's shirt sleeve trying to get his brother to sit down. But Charlie was on a roll.

"Hell-fire, Judge. Five hundred dollars can't touch the contempt I have for this damn court!"

Harting shook his head as he said, "Fine, Mr. Kincade. Let's try three thousand dollars, then."

Jack turned to Charlie. "Please, Uncle Charlie. Sit down before you end up in a cell yourself."

Charlie's eyes were filled with fire. He raised his arm to say something again, but the judge brought the gavel up at the same time. Holding it there in mid-air waiting for Charlie to open his mouth one more time. For a few seconds it was a Mexican standoff.

"Jesus, Charlie! Sit the hell down will you?" pleaded Richard. "Talk about an alligator mouth! Three thousand dollars—Jesus Christ! Sit your butt down!"

Judge Harting had won the war as Charlie silently lowered his arm and sat down. Placing the gavel to the side, the judge asked Jack if he had made his decision.

This time there was no hesitation in the young man's voice. "Your honor, I would consider it an honor and a privilege to serve in the United States Army, and thank you, Sir."

The crack of the gavel ended any further discussion on the matter as Judge Harting pronounced, "This court is adjourned."

Everyone stood as Judge Harting left the room. Agent Jackson, clearly disgusted with the outcome, paused as he was passing Jack. "We had you kid. You might have got away this time, but I know your kind. You can fool that damn judge, but you're not fooling me. You'll be running again—and I'll be waiting for you. I'm going to put you away, kid—you think about that."

Rich and Charlie eyed the agent hard as Jackson finished his threat and walked away. "Jesus, Rich, I don't even know that guy, but you'd think we'd been enemies for years."

"You made him look like a fool. Gives you a good idea the kinda man your daddy was up against with that damn Sheriff Jennings," said Charlie.

The bailiff approached the group. "Mr. Kincade, you'll have to come to the judge's chambers to pay your contempt fine. Follow me please."

The trio followed the man to Harting's office. As they entered, the judge was hanging his black robe in a closet as he said, "Thank you, Josh. That'll be all."

The bailiff closed the door as he nodded and left the room.

"Sit down, gentlemen."

The Kincades moved to the chairs that surrounded a huge cherry-wood desk that consumed most of the room. Charlie had already pulled his checkbook from his pocket and was searching for a pen when the judge said, "You won't need that, Charlie. The fine was for the benefit of Mr. Jackson."

The brothers glanced at each other questionably and shrugged.

"You boys don't remember me, do you?" asked Harting, as he lit a cigar.

Rich shook his head. "I'm afraid you've got us at a disadvantage here, your honor."

Harting smiled. "Well, I suppose moving down a mountain at close to a hundred miles an hour, it's rather hard to see who's chasing you in that rearview mirror."

"Harting," muttered Charlie. "Where have we heard that name before, Rich?"

Both men were quiet for a moment. Deep in thought.

"Oh, I doubt you boys would remember the name. I was just another one of Bill Jennings's lowly deputies back in those days."

This remark brought young Jack upright in his chair,

and a frown to the faces of the uncles. Of course, the judge had expected this type of reaction and quickly continued, "Jennings hired me on after I got out of the army in '62. I was twenty-six then and thought I knew how to drive until I chased you boys a few times. Never could get that damn bootlegger's spin of yours right. But I sure did a lot of three-sixties."

Charlie eyed the judge hard as he asked, "Just how'd one of Jennings's step-and-fetch-it boys get to be a judge?" There was no mistaking the sarcasm in his voice as he asked the question.

Harting didn't seem offended by the remark. "First of all, Charlie, when you're fresh out of the army, want to get married, and need a job as bad as I did, you step and fetch for whoever and whenever you're told to. I worked as a deputy at night and went to college during the day. I was determined I was going to get a law degree and one day be a judge. It took a hell of a lot of work and effort, but here I am. And another thing—just because I worked for Jennings, doesn't mean I liked the son of a bitch!"

Jack leaned forward in his chair. He couldn't help himself. He had to know. "Judge Harting. Were you there? I mean, that night, when it happened."

The room became as quiet as a tomb for a few moments. The judge nodded, "Yes, Jack. I'm sorry to say, I was. It's been over seventeen years and I can still see your dad, all shot up on the ground next to that coal black Chevy of his, and that damn Jennings still shooting at him." Harting paused a second, staring silently down at the desktop before he continued, "I'll never forget the sound of Jennings screaming when he was engulfed in that God-awful inferno. Yeah, I was there all right, Jack. A part of me will always be there. I quit the next day— turned in my badge and gun and simply walked away."

Jack had other questions he wanted to ask, but abandoned the idea when he saw the pained expression of anguish the memory brought to the judge's face. There was another moment of silence before Richard said, "We'd really like to thank you for helping Jack out of this jam, Your Honor. I really mean that."

"I figured that was the least I could do given the circumstances of the past. But Jack, you're going to have to join the army. You better believe that fellow, Jackson, will be watching to see that you do," said Harting.

Jack was more relaxed as he replied, "It's a lot better than jail, your honor. Thank you for giving me a break."

The judge laughed, "Let's see if you still feel that way when those drill sergeants start rolling you out of bed at four thirty every morning."

It was a mixed bag of emotions on the drive home. There was relief that Jack was not in jail and had an opportunity to wipe the whole incident out as if it had never happened. But on the other hand, there was a subdued sadness. Judge Harting's decision meant that Jack would be leaving home. There wouldn't be another racing season for him, at least for the next three years. Even on the ride home, his uncles kept trying to think of another way of handling the situation, but there just were no other options. If there had been, they felt certain that Judge Harting would have found another way.

They had talked about the judge and Jack had caught another butt-chewing from Charlie on the way out of Charlotte, but now, as they neared home, Jack was starting to worry. What was he going to tell his mother? She had tried her best to keep Jack from falling under the influences of the past. Always praising his father, but at the same time driving home the point that living such a life could only lead to trouble, or worse. She had put all her energy into raising her son to be hard-working, honest and forthright. Jack realized that the events of the last twenty-four hours would leave her heartbroken and devastated, and that hurt him more than the threat of jail or the verbal abuse from Charlie ever could.

Charlie and Rich felt certain they could somehow keep Claire from finding out about what had happened. Jack wasn't as sure. As much as he hated the idea of lying to his mother, it seemed a lot better than the alternative. Maybe they were right. Maybe she would never find out, but that was only one of the problems. Telling her he was leaving was going to be even harder to explain. Jack couldn't remember ever saying a single thing about the United States Army in any discussion he'd ever had with his mother. Now, like a bolt from the blue, he'd decided he was going to join the military. How was he going to explain this sudden surge of patriotism. She knew how much he loved racing and traveling with his uncles. And this year he was actually going to get a chance to drive in some of those races. Now, she was supposed to believe that he'd decided to dump all that to join the army? Charlie and Rich were at a loss as to how he was going to explain that one. He'd just have to handle it as best he could.

As the trio made their way up the mountain, Jack started to point out the turn-off to the load point where he had left his car.

"No need for that Jack. Charlie and I have made more trips down that road than we care to remember."

Driving down the back road, Jack halfway expected to see a crusty old fellow with salt and pepper hair step out of the woods with his sawed-off shotgun and confront them, but there was no one around as they pulled into the clearing. Jack's black Trans Am sat where he had left it in the shadows of the tall pines. It was the only vehicle around. Howie Price's pick-up was already gone. Jack wasn't sure if Howie had completed his run and got back early, which was doubtful, or if someone had drove it home for him. Charlie had told Jack about Howie's call and the fact that he had fired the man before he got off the phone. In his defense, Jack had tried to get Charlie to reconsider that decision. After all, it was Jack that had begged and pleaded with the man to let him make the run that night. Somehow it just didn't seem right that Howie should lose his job over a bad decision that Jack himself had made. But Charlie wouldn't give an inch on the subject. One of the primary reasons Charlie paid his mechanics so well was so they wouldn't have to resort to illegal whiskey running. He wanted to keep them out of that business for good. He knew all too well the hardships that prison life placed on both the tripper and his family. It not only caused trouble for the men that did it, but brought his business under suspicion as well. No, Howie had made his decision. He knew the rules. Even if Jack hadn't been involved, Charlie would have fired him or any other employee he discovered dealing with illegal whiskey. One stay in a federal prison had been enough for Charlie Kincade and he wasn't about to do another because of the actions of someone else.

As the three men walked to Jack's car, Charlie asked, "You got your keys, boy?"

Jack pulled them from his pocket and held them up. It wasn't until that moment that he realized his hand was shaking. He couldn't explain it. Maybe it was the realization of how close he had come to going to prison. Maybe it was the idea of having to face his mother and lie. Or perhaps, because it was here, at this very spot, he'd made a decision that could have changed his entire life.

Charlie slapped him on the shoulder. "Jack, my boy. You're damn lucky is all I can say. You dodged a bullet this time. I don't want there to be a second—you understand what I'm sayin'?"

Jack nodded, as he quickly replied, "Loud and clear, Uncle Charlie. You have my word on that."

Charlie squeezed the boy's shoulders. "That's good enough for me. If man ain't got nothin' else, he's at least got his word. An' that's worth more than money any day."

"Damn straight about that," added Rich, as he stepped forward and slapped Jack on the butt. "Now get home and see your mom."

Jack watched them drive out of the clearing, grateful for the fact that they had always been there for him and his mother. Charlie was right. He was damn lucky. Lucky to have people like them that cared for him.

Rolling down the window on the Trans Am, Jack cranked the big V-8 to life, easing the car across the clearing and onto the dirt road that would take him back to the highway. Jack glanced back at the clearing as it disappeared in his sideview mirror. He wasn't only leaving behind a bad decision, but a man wandering the woods with a sawed-off shotgun and a kid's foolish idea that there was something exciting and adventurous about running moonshine.

9

Within a month of Judge Harting's decree, Jack Kincade was bound for Fort Benning, Georgia, and Army Basic Training. It had taken Jack a full week to convince his mother that his sudden urge to join the army and see the world was purely one of his own choosing and something he felt "he had to do."

Of course this decision had the full backing of his uncles, who had worked round the clock to conceal the truth from his mother, while taking every opportunity to herald the various advantages of Jack's "wise decision." "It would be good for the boy and build character as well."

Judge Harting had been right about one thing. The drill sergeants certainly gave Jack reason to consider whether or not he had made the correct decision—especially at 04:30 every morning, when they were awakened by bright overhead lights and the booming, almost thunderous, voices of the drills screaming for them to "hit the floor running." Still, as loud and rowdy as it sometimes seemed, it was a damn sight better than being in a federal prison.

The first few weeks had been the roughest for Jack. He quickly discovered that everything in the military was strictly regimented and on a strict time schedule. When to eat, when to sleep, when to drill and when to speak. But he learned that he wasn't the only one struggling to deal with this new form of culture shock. Everyone that had arrived with him was in the same boat. They came from every part of the nation: north, south, east and west. African Americans, Mexicans, Native Americans, Yankees and Southern boys, all gathered for the great adventure of military life. Jack soon discovered that he was not the only one to be offered a choice between military time or jail time. However, Jack's case was unique—he was the only one there for running illegal whiskey. He was a real-life "Moonshiner," a title that instantly brought him a measure of respect from a number of his peers.

Like so many of the others, Jack believed himself to be in pretty good shape physically when he arrived at basic training. But the drills quickly dispelled that myth. By the end of the third week, they had weeded out those that could not adapt to the rigid requirements of an American soldier. Many were lost for physical reasons, while others found that they could not handle the strict discipline the system required. Still others simply took off at the first opportunity, forever branded deserters.

Jack could understand the physical failures and even the disciplinary problems, but for the life of him, he couldn't understand how anyone could simply quit and run away, knowing that they would forever be listed as a deserter from the United States Army. Although the military no longer pursued them as they had in the past, a deserter would have to live out the rest of his life looking over his shoulder, never quite sure when or where his secret might suddenly be revealed.

Of the 120 men that had formed Jack's company in the beginning, only ninety-four remained at the end of the sixth week. Thanks to the hard work and determination of the drill sergeants, those ninety-four were becoming a well-trained, well-disciplined unit that not only worked well together, but now demonstrated a new spirit and respect for themselves.

Jack had never felt more alive or physically fit as he did going into the final two weeks of basic. His six-foot-two frame had filled out and he weighed two hundred pounds—all of it solid muscle. Along with the newfound confidence the military had provided had come new-found friends. Among these were two with whom Jack had developed a close friendship. Not only because they were likable fellows, but because they also shared a common interest: cars, speed and racing.

Deke Turner was a tall Texas cowboy with fiery red hair and a Texas twang to his voice that came straight out of the old West. Jack likened him to a redheaded Gary Cooper. He had that Cooper walk and answered practically every question with a simple, "Yep" or "Nope." Deke could tell you who had won every Daytona 500 since its conception, as well as the make and model of the car that won the race.

Another close friend was Tyrell Davis, a husky-built black soldier from a little town outside of New Orleans. Tyrell had proven to be the super soldier of the company. Highly intelligent and physically tough, he had easily swept the top honors in the P.T. competition, placed first in the rifle and marksmanship competition, attained the rank of acting platoon sergeant and compiled a total score of 98 percent on the written proficiency exams that covered every phase of training to date. It was for these reasons that Tyrell was presented the Commander's Trophy for Super Soldier of the command.

Interestingly enough, this was a friendship that had

begun as a result of a fight. Even though it was the 1980s and the military was a multicultural organization, there was still a sense of racism lying just below the surface, and it wasn't restricted primarily to good ol' Southern boys, as was the popular belief of many people. Jack had quickly learned that when racism raised its ugly head, there were no boundaries.

Jack had taken notice of Tyrell in those first few days of basic, primarily because of his size and athletic ability. Other than that he was just another member of the company. During their three weeks of training, Jack and Deke returned from a late-night supply detail, when they heard what unmistakably were the sounds of a brawl going on behind one of the barracks buildings. As they made their way around the corner of the building, they found six white soldiers from another company surrounding a black soldier who stood in the center of the circle.

Jack and Deke saw that it was Tyrell. There were signs of blood around his mouth and a small stream flowing from above his left eye. As his attackers moved around him, Tyrell was wiping at the bleeding eye and at the same time, smiling as he taunted his attackers. "If that's the best you boys got, you better go back and get some more help!"

A tall, wiry, blonde-headed boy, the obvious leader of the group, sneered as he replied, "Go on, boy! Talk that crap! You know what we're gonna' do? We're gonna' kick the shit out of your black ass, then we're gonna' cut your fuckin' balls off. What'd you think of that?"

Tyrell never wavered. "I think that's pretty damn big talk comin' from a pencil-necked, little dick, mother-fucker—that's what I think!"

The talking was over. As the circle began to close in on Tyrell, the night air was broken by a high-pitched rebel yell and a rowdy Texas "Yahoo" as Jack and Deke charged out of the darkness and piled into the circle of attackers. Fist and feet were flying in all directions, with the newcomers taking full advantage of the element of surprise.

Jack quickly dropped two of the attackers, one with a knee to the groin and a second with a bone-jarring elbow blow to the side of the head. Tyrell had suddenly reached out with his big hands and grabbed Pencil-neck by the front of the shirt and pulling him forward toward him, head-butted the leader across the bridge of the nose. The sound of shattering bone followed in the waves of screaming pain as the loudmouth dropped like a rock to the ground.

Deke had a guy in a headlock and another guy hung around his neck when Tyrell reached forward and jerked the man off Deke's back. The Texas boy glanced up at Tyrell and with a wink and a smile, said, "Thanks, partner," then continued driving his fist into the face of the head he still held firmly locked in the crook of his arm.

By the time the dust settled, two of Tyrell's tormentors had run off and the remaining four were sprawled motionless on the ground at his feet. Brushing himself off, Deke grinned as he said, "Damn Tyrell, I ain't had so much fun since the pigs ate my sister."

Jack stepped forward and took a look at the cut over Tyrell's eye. "You could use a stitch or two over that eye."

Tyrell shook his head. "That's okay. I've had worse."

Deke reached out a handkerchief which Tyrell gladly accepted, and pressed it into place on the cut.

"I want to thank you both," said Tyrell. "They came at me two at a time at first, but when they saw that wasn't going to get the job done, they decided there was power in numbers. Pencil-neck was right about one thing. They would have kicked my ass good if you fellows hadn't come along when you did. Thanks again."

Tyrell paused a moment, as if trying to remember

something, then looking toward Jack, asked, "You're Kincade. The moonshiner, right?"

Jack nodded, "Yeah, Jack Kincade. And this red-headed cowboy here is—"

Tyrell grinned a broad smile as he cut Jack off. "Yeah—Deke Turner, right?"

"Yep."

As the victims on the ground began to moan and slowly start to move around, Jack asked, "You want to wait around for these guys to get up and see if they want to play some more or head for the barracks?"

Tyrell stared down at them, then shook his head. "No, I think I've had about all the fun I can stand for one night. We better get back and hit the rack."

And so it was that a close and lasting friendship had been formed that night among three soldiers from three different parts of the country. The following day they discovered they had even more in common. They learned that Tyrell's father owned his own garage in New Orleans and that Tyrell had been working on engines since the age of twelve. From that time on the three were inseparable. If you wanted to join in on their conversations, you had better know something about cars, motors or racing. Otherwise, you were nothing more than an observer. Even those that thought they knew a lot about cars soon discovered they were totally out of their league with these three.

As the final two weeks before graduation from basic approached, the men of the company began receiving their orders for their next assignments, where they would receive advanced training in their selected fields. Jack had followed his uncle's advice and selected mechanic's school. It was something he knew and would land him a plush job in a motor pool where he was sure to gain immediate recognition and promotion.

Tyrell's father had offered his son the same advice,

with the idea that Tyrell would return home after the service and take over the family business. Deke, on the other hand, had opted for the more adventurous field of Combat Infantry. Jack and Tyrell were certain that their friend had grown up watching entirely too many John Wayne movies, and were constantly kidding him about that fact. They were hardly surprised when he walked in one day and stated that he was not only going to be an infantryman but an airborne ranger as well. He had just signed up for the grueling three-week airborne course which was conducted on the other side of the base. He would start training immediately after graduation.

The three of them had toured the airborne area one weekend while on pass. They had stood at the base of one of the 250-foot towers from which the trainees were dropped for practice. Just looking up that high had given both Jack and Tyrell a sick feeling in the pit of their stomachs. They couldn't imagine jumping out of a perfectly good airplane at 1200 feet. They were convinced that Deke was out of his mind. There was no way they would ever consider such a harebrained idea.

The trio were on the last pass before graduation week and having a beer at one of the clubs just off post. While Deke and Tyrell shot a game of pool, Jack was at a table reading the last letter he had received from his mother. She had written him faithfully every week since he had been gone, as had both Rich and Charlie. Like any serviceman, Jack was always glad to receive their letters, but likewise, after reading them he couldn't help but get a little homesick.

According to the folks back home, everything was going pretty well. Charlie and Rich were back on the circuit and had won or placed in four of their last nine races. They had tried to get Claire to go with them and the families to a few of the local races, but Jack's mom still refused. Speed and cars had killed her husband. She had no desire to attend an affair where a crowd of people cheered for such things.

Charlie's letters were always so upbeat and positive. He was continuously bragging on Jack and how, if Jack were driving one of their cars, they'd win every race on the circuit. Other than his mother, that was what Jack missed the most, the good times he'd had at the different tracks with his two uncles. This year would have been his chance to be driving on those tracks, shooting the gap, drafting for the lead and the checkered flag. But no, instead he was drinking a beer in a bar in Columbus, Georgia. What was worse was the fact that he had nobody to blame for his situation but himself, and he knew that. Charlie had mentioned in his letter that they were going to be running in the Heritage 100 late-model stocks at Columbus in a few weeks. But Jack would already be gone by then. He and Tyrell both had orders for Fort Dix, New Jersey, and the army motor mechanics school. Fort Dix of all places. The thought was too depressing to think about. Laying the letter aside, Jack finished his beer and ordered another one. He was still in the throes of depression when Deke and Tyrell finished their game and came back to the table. .

"Wooo, what have we here, Tyrell?" said Deke with a grin. "This ol' boy looks like he just lost his best huntin' dog and a girlfriend all in the same day."

"What's wrong, Jack?" asked Tyrell.

Jack slowly turned the beer bottle in his hand as he answered, "Oh, nothing, really."

"Well it's sure as hell got to be somethin', partner. Ain't nobody gets a droopy lookin' face like that from good news," said Deke.

Jack tapped the piece of paper on the table. "It's this letter I got from my uncle Charlie. They're going to be racing in the Heritage 100 here in Columbus the end of next month and I'll be at Fort Dix, New Jersey. Hell, they'll be racing all over the South: Georgia, Alabama, South Carolina, and I'll be in New Jersey, damn it. Fat chance I can get out of there to make any of those races."

There was silence around the table for a moment, then Deke lowered his beer and while staring at the topless dancer on the stage across the room, he uttered, "It don't have to be that way, Jack."

Jack glanced up at his friend. "What'd you mean, Deke?"

Deke's eyes were fixed on the young woman's breasts as she swayed to the music coming from the jukebox. "Mercy sakes alive. I swear, that gal's hooters defy all the known principles of gravity."

Jack leaned forward on the table. "Deke! What do you mean, it don't have to be that way?"

Deke managed to divert his eyes long enough to look at Jack. "It's simple, partner. You just go over to the personnel office Monday morning and tell 'em you want to volunteer for Airborne school, then Ranger school. I know for a fact that the Rangers are short on recruitment this month and they're snappin' up anybody that'll volunteer. They even got two of their own guys workin' over there to handle all the necessary order changes. They can get it done in a day."

Jack slumped back in his chair, surprised that Deke could even suggest such a thing. Jump out of an airplane—no way.

Tyrell downed a shot of his beer and laughed. "Tell you this boy was one brick short of a load, Jack. Can you imagine—giving up a plush motor pool job for a chance to fall out of the sky and wander around the swamps at night with a hundred pounds of shit on your back. Gotta' be Texas's idea of havin' a damn good time."

Deke's eyes were back on the dancer. "Go ahead and laugh. But Airborne school is three weeks long, say another week or two after that before I start Ranger school, that's twelve more weeks, then a couple more weeks waiting for orders. I'd say that guarantees me maybe five months before I have to leave good old Fort Benning and the lovely ladies of Columbus for anywhere else—especially Fort fuckin' Dix, New Jersey."

Jack was still silent, but his mind wasn't. He found himself actually considering what Deke had just said. He was right about one thing. Both schools were taught at Fort Benning. He wouldn't have to leave Columbus for at least five months, and there were bound to be breaks between the schools and on weekends. He could actually go to some of the races and maybe even get home a couple of times. It really wasn't that far from Columbus to Charlotte, but from New Jersey—forget it.

Tyrell set his beer down and looked long and hard at Jack before he said, "Uh oh, I don't like what I see goin' on over there, Jack. Don't tell me you're actually thinking about what this cowboy's just said."

The dancer suddenly forgotten, Deke turned to look at Jack. There was a smile on his face as he waited to see what his friend was going to say.

"Deke, you think they'd take me at Ranger school?" asked Jack.

"Without a doubt, partner."

"But I've got to go Airborne?"

"First requirement. No Airborne—no Ranger."

Now it was Tyrell's turn to lean back in his chair. "I don't believe I'm hearing this bullshit. You're both nuts!"

Deke and Jack smiled at one another, then at Tyrell, who quickly grabbed his beer and downed the whole thing in one long gulp. Setting the bottle down, he shook his head, "Oh no you don't. You ain't gettin' me involved in this bullshit. No fuckin' way, brother!"

First thing Monday morning, Jack was at the personnel section. At the mention of the word Ranger, a young sergeant jumped up from his desk and told the clerk at the counter that he would handle things for Jack. Within ten minutes everything was taken care of and the necessary paperwork signed.

Reaching out his hand to Jack, the sergeant grinned as he said, "Congratulations, Private Kincade. Glad to have you with us."

After a firm handshake, the sergeant placed a new set of papers on the counter then asked, "And you, Private. What's your name?"

"Davis—Tyrell Davis."

10

"Ladies and gentlemen, welcome to the Heritage 100 and the Grady Speedway in beautiful Columbus, Georgia. We expect to begin the late-model qualifying runs within the hour. In the meantime, feel free to avail yourself of your favorite food or drink at the many various concession stands located throughout the speedway area. We ask that you please avoid the race-car area at the north end of the track where the teams are in the process of preparing for the upcoming time trials. Your cooperation is appreciated. Enjoy yourselves and get ready for some of the finest racing in the South—thank you."

Deke was following close behind Jack and Tyrell as they made their way through the crowd and headed for the north end of the field. "You hear what that announcer said, Jack?"

"Yeah," answered Jack, "But that don't apply to us, Deke. We're related to one of the teams."

Tyrell laughed, "You're going to be hard-pressed to convince those security boys that I'm part of your family, Jack."

Jack was about to come back with a remark of his own, when suddenly he spotted Charlie and Rich near one of the car haulers. Although he'd only been gone three months, to Jack, seeing his uncles now, it suddenly seemed like he'd been gone for years. There was no containing his excitement. "There they are!" he yelled, pointing to a double-decker car hauler adorned in red, white, and blue.

Jack was yelling to Charlie and waving his arms to try and get his uncle's attention when his legs suddenly came into contact with a white, steel pipe and chain-link fence that surrounded the team area. An army of security people dressed in blue jeans and black T-shirts patrolled the line, stopping anyone trying to enter the restricted area. The trio were wearing their uniforms and the moment Jack swung his spit-shined jump boot up on the pipe to go over the fence, three security men quickly appeared in front of him. Pushing the boot off the rail, the largest of the three asked, "And just where the hell you think you're goin' there, soldier boy?"

Jack caught himself on the rail to keep from falling and eyed the security man with a look that was anything but friendly.

"The Kincade brothers are my uncles and I intend to go over there and see them. You got a problem with that?"

Eyeing the jump wings on Jack's chest, the security man said, "Look, Airborne. Just cause you say it, don't make it so. I could say I'm Dale Earnhart, but it don't make no difference. Our orders are to keep everybody back. And nobody passes this fence. Now move along before there's trouble."

The remark seemed to ignite a fire in the newly christened airborne troopers. Tyrell moved closer to the rail, "You better get yourself some more help if you think there's going to be a problem. You three sure as hell won't be any trouble."

Tensions suddenly accelerated a notch as people who had been gathered at the rail began to move away from the troopers and the security men, fully expecting things to explode into an all-out brawl at any time. There was an awkward moment of silence as the combatants stared across the railing at one another, each waiting for the other to make the first move. Just as it seemed the action was about to start, a voice from somewhere behind the security men said, "Jack Kincade—I should have known there'd be a Kincade involved in that trouble call I just received."

The security men stepped aside, allowing their boss to approach the railing. The man's face seemed familiar, but Jack couldn't place him.

"Don't remember me, do you son?" said the middle-aged man.

Jack shook his head. "No, sir, I'm sorry, but I don't."

The man smiled. "You'd think a fellow would remember the name of a guy he got fired from his last job. It's Jake—Jake Dunn. Last year—Elmore City race. Track down at Macon. You and your uncles won the trophy and kicked the hell out of an ol' boy named Weaver and his crew."

Jack clearly remembered now. "Didn't know you lost your job over that, Mr. Dunn. I'm sorry."

Dunn laughed, "Hell, don't apologize, son. Best damn thing that ever happened to me, really. Got this job as chief of security here. Hell, it pays three times the money and comes without all the bullshit I had to put up with back in Macon."

Dunn reached out and shook hands with Jack. The grip was firm and friendly. "Joined the army since I saw you last—and Airborne too. Damn good choice. Served with the Eighty-second All-American myself. Guess you're wanting to see Charlie and Rich. That right?"

"Yes, sir. They don't know I'm here. I'd kind of like to surprise them."

Jake stepped back from the railing. Waving his security men away, he told their leader, "I'll take care of this, you boys go on back to work. Come on, Jack. I'll walk over with you."

The three troopers were over the rail in a bound and followed Jake to the Kincade garage area. Near the doors, Jake told Jack and the others to wait behind the doors, he'd be right back. Jack wasn't sure what Jake was up to, but he seemed like a nice enough fellow. They'd do as he asked.

When Dunn walked into the garage, he saw Charlie and Rich checking the tire pressure on the stack of spares. As he drew closer, he yelled, "Hey, Rich, Charlie. They need to see you at the qualifiers' booth."

The brothers walked up to Jake. "What's the trouble, Dunn? We got work to do here."

Dunn shook his head. "Ya' got me, boys. Seems somebody's filed a complaint against you. Something about an illegal engine or something."

Rich threw down his tire gauge and Charlie, his face turning red as fire, shouted, "What low-life son of a bitch said that? I'll kick his ass all the way to Alabama!"

Dunn was trying hard to keep a straight face.

"Yeah! Where's the bastard that filed that complaint?" snarled Richard.

"He's right outside," said Dunn, "if you want to take it up with him. But I'd walk soft if I were you. Boy's got some friends with him, and they look pretty tough."

"Shit!" cried Charlie, picking up a tire iron. "We can even it up pretty damn quick. Come on, Rich."

Jake Dunn was grinning as the brothers stormed outside, ready to take on who or whatever was waiting for

them. Charlie was huffing and puffing like an old bear
with a bad tooth as he exited the garage and began looking around for his adversary, with Rich close behind.

"Hey old man! You lookin' to Jack somebody up?"

The brothers twirled to face the voice that had come
from behind them. The fierceness quickly disappeared
from their faces, replaced by wide grins as they saw Jack
in his dress green uniform and shining jump boots.

"Well, I'll be damned," cried Charlie. "Will you look
at that, brother? We sent 'em a boy and they done made
a damn good-lookin' soldier out of him. Yes, sir."

Jack stepped forward and hugged both men tightly,
fighting to hold back the tears at seeing them again. Deke
and Tyrell couldn't miss the misty-eyed look they saw in
the uncles' eyes. Jack had said they were a close family
and this scene left no doubt as to the truth of that statement.

Jack quickly introduced his two friends and they all
went into the garage where Jake Dunn was looking over
one of the cars. "Dunn, you're a real horse's ass, you
know that don't ya?" said Charlie, but he was smiling all
the time.

"Yeah, I know," said the security man. "I couldn't
resist it. Makes us even for Macon. Good luck tonight,
Charlie. See you, Jack," said Dunn as he waved good-bye
and went back to work.

Tyrell was bent over the engine in Rich's number
twenty car, a red and blue 1986 Ford Thunderbird, with
the others around the car. "Interested in race cars,
Tyrell?" asked Rich.

"Tyrell's dad owns a garage in New Orleans. Ty
started as a mechanic when he was twelve," said Jack.

"That's right," Tyrell said. "Been around cars and
motors all my life. Never really thought much about racing them. I figured it cost a small fortune to get into it."

Charlie gave a short laugh as he said, "Ain't nothin'

small about it, Tyrell. It costs a hell of a lot of money these days. And, brother, if you don't win or place once in a while, it'll put a guy in the poor house, damn quick."

Tyrell studied the engine for a moment. "Runnin' a 358-cubic-inch V-8 with a two-barrel, probably get one hundred thirty to one hundred forty miles per hour out of her. A four-barrel carb would get one hundred fifty to maybe one hundred sixty wide open on a one-mile concrete track—not so sure about asphalt. Might be too many horses for the curves."

Everyone stared at Tyrell in stunned silence for a moment. "Thought you didn't care much for racin'," said Charlie.

"No, Sir, said I never thought much about it. That was, until I met Jack and Deke here. Been doing a little reading up on it since then. Now that we've been to a couple of races, it looks like it might be fun. How many cars you running tonight?" asked Tyrell.

"Just two," said Rich. "This Ford and Charlie's favorite, a 1987 Monte Carlo SS Aero Coup. Of course you boys will want to be on the infield during the race. You'll get a hell of a view of the action from out there."

"That'd be great," said Deke. "Get a better view of the hooters from there, too."

The brothers shot a questionable glance at the trooper from Texas before Jack said, "Don't mind Deke. He has this fixation with tits."

"Hell, who don't!" laughed Charlie as he closed the hood down on the Ford.

While the brothers moved the cars toward the track for the qualifying laps, Jack and the others moved out onto the infield. Woody Clark, Charlie's pit boss, had his RV parked near the Kincade brothers' pit area. Three lawn chairs and a cooler of ice-cold beer lined the top of the expensive motor home.

Deke was the last to climb the side ladder to the roof.

Once on top he let out a Texas yell then shouted, "Boys, this is what I call a class operation. We got the best seats in the house."

No one could argue with that. From their vantage point they could see all 360 degrees of the track. Passing out the beer, Jack noticed that Charlie had set a pair of binoculars next to one of the chairs. A small note attached read, "For the hooters fan—happy viewing."

Jack and Tyrell were laughing as they passed the glasses to Deke, who immediately turned them toward the Kincade cars being rolled out to the line. Spying Charlie looking their way, Deke raised his beer in a salute to the man, who in turn acknowledged with a snappy salute of his own to his nephew's newfound friends.

In the qualifying rounds, Charlie set a pace that earned him a fourth-place position on the pole. Rich didn't fare as well, ending up toward the rear of the pack at number eighteen on the outside. By the time the main event began there were forty-four drivers following the pace car around the track, picking up speed as they rounded the third turn, then suddenly, the pace car shot forward and quickly exited the track. The field of cars all seemed to lunge forward at the same time, the roar of the mighty engines drowning out the wild cheers of the crowd that numbered close to eighteen thousand.

Jack and Tyrell were on their feet, caught up in the excitement and cheering Charlie and Rich on as they made the first turn. Deke was equally excited; field glasses in hand he had zeroed in on a red halter top and was closely following every bounce the young blonde wearing it made as she jumped up and down.

By the time they had reached the half-way point of seventy-five laps, seventeen cars had been eliminated, either by crashes, blown engines, or overheated motors. Charlie had been holding his own throughout the race and was still in fourth place after having dropped back six positions earlier, but fighting his way back to the front pack following an earlier yellow caution. Rich on the other hand was having all kinds of problems. He had barely missed becoming tangled up in the first major crash of the night, and now his Ford was running hot and he was falling farther and farther back in the pack.

It all came to an end for Richard on lap 102. He had accelerated coming out of turn two, when he heard a loud *bang* and a cloud of white smoke rolled out from behind the car—the T-bird engine had blown. Rich managed to get the Ford off the track and coast the dead machine to within a few feet of the pit. Woody and the pit crew quickly pushed it out onto the infield to get it out of Charlie's way if he needed the pit before the race was over. Hopefully, he wouldn't have to. They had already put on a new set of tires during a caution on lap ninety-five and topped off the gas tank. Barring any accidents, that should be enough to finish the race.

Jack and Tyrell were on their feet watching Charlie come out of a turn, when Rich came up the ladder to join them.

"Tough luck, Mr. Kincade," said Tyrell. "What happened?"

Rich was almost yelling to be heard over the roar of the cars circling the track, "Think we had a leak in a head gasket. Had me running red-line. Then we lost a cylinder on that last turn—that was all she could stand—she blew."

"Charlie's hanging in there, Rich," said Jack, his voice filled with the familiar excitement Rich had heard so many times.

By lap 139, there were only nineteen cars remaining on the track. Charlie had moved up to third place, twice, then dropped back to fifth, then back into third by the time they completed lap 146. With only four laps left to go, even Deke was on his feet. The hooter section forgotten for the moment, he was cheering along with the rest of them. The RV was literally rocking from side to side as the cheering section jumped up and down on the top, screaming for Charlie to go for broke.

For a moment it looked as if he might have a chance to catch the leader on the first turn of the last lap, but that thought quickly faded as Charlie went too high into the second turn, losing his advantage and falling all the way back to fifth place and finishing the race in that position.

The cheering had stopped now and Rich shook his head. He knew that was a mistake Charlie wouldn't have made a few years ago. But both of them were getting older and a 150-lap race was rough on a young guy, let alone two old men.

"Sorry, Rich," said Jack.

"Awh, hell, Jack," said his uncle, slapping him on the back, "we still get money for fifth place and points for the laps completed. That's what counts right now. It's still early in the season."

After the cars and equipment were loaded, Woody and the crew headed the trailers and RV for home while Rich and Charlie stayed behind. They were taking Jack and his friends out to eat. They had a lot of catching up to do.

The group went to a place called The Black Angus, a popular steak house located outside the gates of Fort Benning. The brothers besieged the boys with questions about airborne school and jumping out of airplanes—and why in the world were they going to Ranger school? And what had happened to the idea of a plush motor-pool job?

As soon as the boys had explained the reasoning behind their decisions, the Kincade brothers found themselves equally besieged by a set of rapid-fire questions from Deke and Tyrell about moonshine-running and bootlegging in the old days. All in all it had turned out to be a pretty good day. Before long, Deke and Tyrell thanked Charlie and Rich for the great seats at the race and the fine dinner, then excused themselves to head back to the base.

"Nice friends you got there, Jack," said Rich, as he watched the two troopers walk out the door.

"Yeah, we've been through a lot together."

Charlie lit a cigarette and leaned back in the booth as he asked, "What happened, Jack? I mean, all this Airborne Ranger stuff. Why the change—really?"

Jack grinned, "Oh, I don't know, Charlie. Started out as a way to stay in Georgia—watch you guys race tonight and maybe get home a few times over the next few months. But once I got into it I found that I really liked it. Being a paratrooper and a Ranger's not like the regular army. You develop something special, you know—a bond, a certain closeness that's not there in the everyday army. You depend on each other and work as a team, kind of like Woody and the crew working the pit—each guy depending on the other guy to hold up his end of the load, and knowing that they can handle anything that comes up. Guess that's why I like it. Working with guys like Deke and Tyrell. We're a team."

Rich took a sip of his coffee and nodded his approval as he said, "We'll have to let Judge Harting know how you're doing. I got a feeling he'll be more than pleased, Jack."

"I hope so. I owe him a lot for giving me this chance," said Jack, who paused a moment then asked, "I know you said Mom was doing fine, but how's she taking my being gone?"

"Oh, you know your mom, Jack," said Charlie. "She could have a railroad spike in her foot and convince ya it wasn't nothin' but a cramp in her big toe. Your ma's not one to complain about things. Last time we saw her, she was doin' fine. Said she was writin' ya every week. One thing certain, she's mighty proud of ya, Jack. Got that picture of ya' graduatin' from Airborne school sittin' right in the center of the mantel over the fireplace. Makes a point of showin' it to everybody that comes by."

Jack's face took on a certain look of sadness. "I shouldn't have lied to her, Charlie. Should have been man enough to tell her the truth—but I just couldn't do it. Figured it would have broke her heart."

Both uncles agreed with that as Rich said, "Maybe after you're out of the army, you can sit her down and explain it all to her. Why you did what you did and how you knew it'd bother her. I'm sure she'd understand, Jack."

The waitress brought another round of coffee as Jack asked when and where their next race was going to be. "The State Farm 200 at Charlotte Motor Speedway, two weeks from today," said Charlie. "Can you and the boys make it?"

"No, afraid not. We'll be in Ranger school by then. This was kind of like our last shot at freedom before the class starts. They say it's a tough twelve weeks, but I don't doubt we can handle it if we stick together. Might be able to come home on leave after we finish the school. Mom'd like that."

"Yeah," muttered Rich, with a concerned look on his face, which did not go unnoticed by Jack.

"What's wrong, Rich? You look worried," Jack asked.

"Awh, it's nothing really. You just be careful, you hear. I've heard stories about these Rangers and special operations and all that kinda' stuff. You and those friends of yours could end up facing the wrong end of a gun or something, you ain't careful."

Charlie shook his head in agreement, "This ol' world's changin' pretty fast, Jack. Ain't no big wars goin' on anymore, but they sure got a shitload of them little ones goin' on in places I never heard of. You sure you wanta' do this Ranger thing?"

"As sure as I've ever been about anything, Charlie.

But you two do me a favor, okay. Don't play up this Ranger business too much around Mom. I don't want her worrying about me any more than she already does."

They all agreed, then spent another hour talking about cars, races, and who they thought would be the toughest competition on the circuit this year. It was well past one in the morning when they parted company in the parking lot of The Black Angus. Jack promised to get home on leave the first chance he had and to bring Deke and Tyrell along if they wanted.

Rich was concerned that they had kept Jack out too long. But he told them not to worry. He had all day Sunday to rest up. Monday morning they would start Ranger school. For Jack it was just another challenge—to Rich and Charlie, it was a sign that the boy they had helped raise as their own, was growing up. His father would have been proud.

11

Ranger school proved to be every bit as tough as people said it was. There were times, midway through the course, that each and every one of the trio felt they weren't going to make it. But each time one of them neared the breaking point—felt he couldn't go on—the other two were there to lend their support and push him that extra mile. It was a sign of true friendship, but better yet, a perfect demonstration of what true comradeship between rangers was all about. By the final week they had survived the rigorous physical training, the treacherous mountain climbing, the two-week survival course in the hazardous swamps of the Florida Everglades and a road march that they swore would have killed an ordinary human being.

It was little wonder that Deke, Tyrell and Jack were proud of their achievement. They had begun Ranger School with a class of 220. On graduation day, they stood on the parade field with ninety-three other proud men that received their coveted black berets. They were full-fledged rangers—among America's elite and best-trained soldiers in the world.

Deke had been right about one thing—their stay at Fort Benning. They were beginning their fifth month there after graduation. In that time, they had managed to make it to three of the Kincade brothers' races: two in Atlanta and the third in Macon. Charlie had totaled his car in the first Atlanta run, but luckily had been able to walk away with only minor cuts and scrapes. Rich had finished fourteenth.

In the second Atlanta run, Rich had lost a transmission midway through the race, but Charlie had finished sixth. It didn't pay a lot of money, but he picked up enough points for the finish to keep himself in the top ten of the point standings, and that was just as important as the money.

Jack was convinced that his uncles had some kind of magical spell on the Macon track. Everything and anything that could go wrong went wrong that night. The qualifying times were terrible, which placed the brothers at the rear of the pack. Thirty minutes before the feature race was to begin, Charlie's fuel pump went out, creating a wild scramble for a replacement and installation. Both Deke and Tyrell figured Charlie was out of the race, but to their amazement, the brothers not only made the race, but finished first and second in a race that saw no less than nine yellow cautions and twenty-three cars knocked out of the event before the checkered flag came down. Afterward, Deke couldn't resist telling the Kincade boys that he hadn't seen any better racing "since the pigs ate my sister!"

Within two weeks after graduation, the newly qualified rangers began to receive their orders. The thought that they may not all get orders to the same duty station never crossed their minds. But that was exactly what happened. Deke was the first to receive his orders. He was being assigned to the 75th Rangers at Fort Lewis, Washington. Jack and Tyrell assumed that their orders would be for the same place. It wasn't until the First Sergeant called them to his office that they realized how wrong they were. Tyrell had impressed the instructors at the Ranger School with his physical stamina and gung-ho attitude—so much so, that they had requested he be assigned to the school as one of their instructors. He wouldn't be leaving Fort Benning and his move would be a short one: from the holding barracks, to the cadre barracks—four blocks down the road.

Jack's orders came as the biggest surprise of all. He'd been assigned to a ranger unit that was presently attached to the Special Warfare Center at Fort Bragg, North Carolina. That put him only two hours from Charlotte and three hours from home. At first he couldn't believe his luck. He had let out a joyful yell and began to dance around the room. It wasn't until he saw the faces of his two friends that he realized what the orders really meant. His happiness over the assignment began to fade when he realized that in less than twenty-four hours, this trio of friends would be going their separate ways. Who knew when they might get together again?

That afternoon the three went back to their rooms and began to pack for their upcoming moves. Once they had everything ready, they met and headed for one of their favorite off-post bars. They knew it would be their last night together. Accordingly, the beer and jokes were practically non-stop. For the most part it was a fun time, with each man trying hard to suppress the sadness they knew they would feel at their eventual departure.

"Hey, Jack. You think you might stay in the Army?" asked Deke.

Jack had to think about that for a minute. This had started out as just something he had to do. But now, after all he'd gone through, he had to admit the army wouldn't be a bad life.

"I can't say right now, Deke. But I've still got a couple of years to make up my mind. How about you, Tyrell?"

The broad-shouldered ranger sat back in his chair. "I gotta' admit, it's a whole different lifestyle, and one I could get used to pretty easy. But my dad's counting on me to take over the business when I finish this tour. Don't think I could let him down."

Deke raised his glass in a toast, "Well, guess that leaves me as the only 'lifer' in the bunch. Here's to the rangers." Tipping the beer up, he drank the entire thing in one long gulp, then set the glass back on the table. "Damn, I love this shit! Airborne!"

"How far?" shouted Tyrell.

"All the way!" came Deke's reply.

The party continued until closing time. Although reluctant for the night to come to an end, the group made their way back to the barracks and some much-needed sleep.

The following morning, Tyrell helped his two friends load their luggage into a car he had rented and drove them to the airport. The luggage unloaded and checked, the three friends stood in silence in front of the airport for a moment. There were suddenly a hundred things they wanted to say or talk about, but now there was no time. Reaching out his hand, Deke said, "Well, Tyrell. You take care of yourself now, you hear."

Tyrell looked down at the outstretched hand. Pushing it aside, he said, "Come here, you redheaded hooter freak." Pulling the Texan to him and hugging him tight, he said, "You know I expect a full report on the hooter situation in Washington, right?"

Deke was slapping Tyrell on the back as he replied, "You know it, partner."

No sooner had Tyrell released Deke, than Jack pulled the big man to him. "Deke's going to be in Washington State, but you're not, mister super troop. So I expect to see you in Charlotte the first chance you get, okay?"

"You got it, Jack," said Tyrell with a broad smile. "Maybe we can talk your uncles into letting us drive for 'em once and awhile."

"Now there's a thought," laughed Deke. "Two guys trained to raise hell and blow shit up, driving thirty-five-thousand-dollar cars at one-forty miles an hour. Now, that's scary."

They were all still laughing as Tyrell got in his car and drove away. Deke and Jack parted company a few minutes later, both promising to stay in touch. One hour later, Jack was on his way to Fort Bragg, and in a way, home.

It took him a week to get situated and processed in at his new duty station. Jack knew right away that he was going to like Fort Bragg. It was the home of the 82nd Airborne Division and the elite Green Berets. He quickly discovered that the Special Warfare Center was, to quote those in the know, "Where the action is." Nearly every member of his ranger detachment had already seen action in a number of out-of-the-way places around the world. And at the rate those small brushfire wars were popping up, it wouldn't be long before Jack could find himself smack in the middle of one of them.

The thought of that both excited and frightened him. How would he react under fire? It was a question every soldier asked himself at one time or another. It was a question to which there was no true answer. Only when the soldier found himself face-to-face with an enemy would he solve the mystery, or die trying.

One month after his arrival at Bragg, Jack requested and was granted a well-deserved two-week leave. The only requirement: he must always have his beeper with him so that he could be recalled at any given moment for immediate deployment, should a situation arise that required his detachment.

His leave papers signed, Jack headed straight for home and a welcome reunion with his mother and his uncles. Jack would always remember the look on his mother's face the day she came to the door and saw her son standing on the porch in his uniform, beret and spit-shined boots. The pride showed in every line of her wonderful face. Although she had never really accepted Jack's reasons for wanting to join the military in the first place, seeing him standing there, no longer as her little boy, but a man—a soldier—the real reason didn't matter anymore.

The experience had changed him, she could see that in his face. But it had been a change for the better. For the first time since Claire could remember, she and her son spent that entire day talking—just talking. And she cherished every moment: the excitement in his voice as he told her about Airborne and Ranger School, his new-found friends and what they were like. Especially pleasing to her was the news that he was stationed only three hours away. That would afford him the opportunity to come home on weekends. They talked late into the night, but she didn't mind; her son was home.

Having spent the weekend with his mother and taking care of a few minor fix-up jobs around the house, Jack headed into Charlotte to see his uncles. He had started to call them when he got home, but sensed that his mother would prefer they spend the weekend together without the distraction of talking about cars and racing. He had guessed right.

As Jack walked into Charlie's garage, the place was filled with cars and everyone was busy as usual. Seeing him enter, the mechanics stopped their work long enough to shake hands with him and welcome him home. Heading to the main office, Jack heard someone shout his name, then say that Charlie and Rich were out back test-running their cars on the short track.

Jack went out the side door of the garage and made his way down to the track fence where he found Woody Clark, the pit boss, with a stopwatch in each hand and a headset with a voice-activated mike on his head. Jack moved up behind the man so quietly that Woody didn't even know he was there. He arrived just in time to hear Woody shouting into the mike, "Damn it Charlie, punch the fuckin' thing will ya! If it blows, we'll rebuild it. So quit babyin' the damn thing."

Jack couldn't help but grin as he thought how sweet it was to hear somebody chewing on Charlie's ass for a change. But from the action on the track it was obvious Charlie didn't react well to criticism. In the blink of an eye, he floored the 1987 Dodge coming out of a turn and fishtailed hard right, then almost lost it as he struggled to correct his mistake. The Dodge slid a good thirty yards sideways before Charlie hit the brake, cut the wheel, and stomped the gas, all in a matter of seconds. The action swung the car a full one-hundred-eighty degrees and propelled him forward again in the center of the track.

While all this was going on, Jack reached for a spare headset that was hanging on the fence. Woody caught the movement out of the corner of his eye and jumped like someone had put a snake in his shorts. "Damn, Jack! Ya could give a guy a heart attack sneakin' up like that."

"Sorry, Woody," he replied, as he slipped the headset on just in time to hear Charlie yelling, "What the hell ya doin' over there Woody? Start me a new time on the next lap. I'm going to open her up this time."

"Roger, you got it Charlie." Woody paused a moment then asked, "How about you, Rich? You want a time lap, too?"

Jack monitored Rich's voice coming back over the headset. He was having a problem with the 1987 Ford he was running through its paces. "No, Woody. I've got something knocking around in the right front and the trans is tight on the shift. I'm bringing her in."

While Rich was easing the Ford off the track, Charlie was building speed for the qualifying run. As he shot past the start gate, Woody clicked the stopwatch. Charlie had the Dodge revved up as tight as he dared on such a short track and he was handling the curves like the old pro he really was, taking them so tight that the dirt was flying thirty feet into the air. When he tore past the gate again, Woody stopped the time and held it up for Jack to see. "14.58—now that's drivin', kid," said Woody. "If only he'd do it like that on race night."

Jack took the headset off. "Maybe you just need to piss him off after the first lap."

Woody cracked a smile. "Maybe you got something there, Jack. I'll have to try that this weekend at Rockingham. Oh, by the way. Good to see ya' home again."

"Thanks, Woody. Guess I'll go in and have a look at Rich's car. See you later."

Rich was already under the Ford inspecting it for the problem when Jack walked up. Kneeling down and glancing under the car he asked, "What'd you do, Rich? Forget to attach one of the shocks?"

Rich raised his head suddenly and bumped it on the frame. "Who the fuck—" Seeing Jack's smiling face staring at him, Rich rubbed his head and laughed. "What the hell would a Ranger know about a shock?"

Wheeling the creeper out from under the car, Rich jumped up, wiped his hands on his jeans, then slapped his nephew on the back. "When'd you get in?"

"Friday night. Spent the weekend with Mom. Just the two of us."

"That's good, Jack. She'd never admit it, but she was really worried about you and how you were doin'. Ya want some coffee?"

"Sure, that sounds good."

The two walked to the main office. While Rich poured, Jack studied the picture of his dad and uncles sitting on the hood of the black 1964 Chevy Impala. They all seemed so young. But by the time that picture had been taken, they had already been running bootleg whiskey for three years.

As Rich and Jack sipped their coffee and talked, Charlie came through the door. His eyes lit up at seeing Jack. When the boy stood, Charlie grabbed him and gave him a big hug, then barked, "Damn boy! Ya done growed a foot and put on twenty pounds since we saw you last." Squeezing Jack's arm, he continued, "An' that's all solid muscle ya got there. This army life must agree with ya."

"Can't complain, Charlie. They keep us in shape and feed us pretty well."

Charlie poured himself a cup of coffee as he asked, "How long ya home for?"

"Couple of weeks," Jack answered.

The brothers exchanged glances before Charlie said, "We got a race comin' up Friday night at Rockingham. Ya wanta drive one of the cars?"

Jack was caught totally off guard by the question. It was something he'd always wanted to do, but figured he'd have to wait until his time in the service was over.

"Well," asked Charlie. "Whaddya say?"

"Sure, I'd like to drive. But will they let me? I mean, I haven't drove a real track race in my life."

Rich got up and moved to the coffee pot for a refill as he said, "Jack, they run a fifty-lap preliminary for amateurs. Standard stocks. It's run before the main feature. That's how a lot of the boys got their start, then worked up to the big stuff. You'll be driving a Kincade car. We're responsible for our cars and the drivers we put in 'em. If we didn't think you could handle it, believe me, we wouldn't put you out on that track."

"Whaddya say, Jack? Ready to start gettin' your feet wet on the racin' circuit?" asked Charlie.

Jack raised his cup as if making a toast. "Sounds like a hell of a plan to me. If you're willing to risk the car and the money, who am I to say no? Let's do it."

Charlie leaned out the door of the office and yelled, "Hey, Larry. Move that number #41 Chevy out to the track, will ya?"

"When we going to get started?" asked Jack.

"Right now," said Charlie with a grin as he set his coffee aside. "You'll practice every day. Give ya' a chance to get used to the feel of the car. Keep in mind that we're not concerned with speed right now, but control—okay?"

Jack was surprised by Charlie's sudden no-nonsense attitude. It was a side of his uncle he'd never seen outside of dealing with his business. But then, that was what racing had become: a business. Oh sure, it was fun for a lot of them, but the bottom line was that it was a business that required a lot of money, a lot of work and a healthy understanding of the real dangers involved. When a lawyer made a mistake and lost a case in court, he could go home, have a drink, write out his bill for some ridiculous amount of money, then forget about it. When a stock-car driver made a mistake at 120 mph, he didn't make any money, he didn't go home, but rather to a hospital, or worse, to the morgue.

Jack spent three hours that first day inspecting every inch of the white 1987 Chevy Monte Carlo with its small block V-8 and rugged suspension that Charlie had picked for him to drive in the Rockingham amateur class. It was a great car as far as Jack was concerned. The big V-8 purred like a kitten, yet had the get-up and go of a tiger. A full hour going around the track gave him a feel for the steering and suspension which made it a snap to handle on the curves, and the shock system was so smooth that it didn't beat a fellow to death. All in all, Jack couldn't have been happier with any other car and told Charlie as much at the end of the day.

"Oh, is that right? She's perfect then. That what you're sayin'?"

"Well, yeah. I guess so, Charlie," was Jack's reply.

"Then why are ya comin' out of the turns so damn high and leavin' yourself open on the low slot?"

Jack suddenly found himself on the defensive. "Well, I . . . I guess I'm just . . ."

Charlie cut him off abruptly. "Ya guess! Ya guess! What the hell kinda answer's that? We don't guess in this business, Jack. Guessin' can get ya killed, or worse, get some other poor bastard killed along with ya."

Thankfully, Rich interceded on Jack's behalf. "Oh, come on, Charlie. Jesus, it's the kid's first day. You act like he ought to know what it took you thirty years to learn. Now back off."

Charlie reluctantly did as his brother asked, but as he was leaving, he muttered, "Okay, but same time tomorrow, and I expect to start seein' some improvements. Good night."

Jack and Rich watched as Charlie closed the door behind him. "Damn, Rich. Was I really that bad out there?"

"No, kid. Matter of fact, you looked pretty good. Of course that old bear would die before he'd tell you that. Not yet anyway."

Jack rubbed the arm of the office chair slowly with his hand as he asked, "Man, Charlie sure has seemed uptight the last few times I've been around. Have I done something, or is there something going on I don't know about, Rich?"

Rich took a bottle of bourbon from the top desk drawer and poured two glasses, handing one to Jack, before he answered.

"I'm not positive, Jack, but I think Charlie's got something wrong with him medically. He says it's just his back, but I'm not so sure."

"Has he been to see the doc about it?"

"Hell, no. Stubborn ol' shit! I'd have a better chance of winning the Indy 500 with a damn Ford Pinto than getting him to a doctor's office. But whatever it is, I'm afraid it's bad and getting worse. Charlie's driving has been pretty erratic at times. I'm getting kind of worried about him."

"So that's it. I thought it was just me."

"Naw, Jack. One thing I do know. That ol' bastard really loves you. He just don't want to see you get hurt. What you saw today was kind of like that tough love thing you hear about these days. Just remember, his bark's a lot worse than his bite."

The two had another drink, then turned out the lights and locked the place up before heading home. Tomorrow was another day.

By Thursday, Jack had mastered both the car and the track. During the week, Charlie had intentionally tampered with the car. The suspension one day; the fuel system the next. Just to see what Jack would do when he experienced the unexpected. On both occasions, Jack had noted the trouble immediately and brought the car off the track the second he detected a problem. This seemed to please Charlie, although he didn't say so in so many words; it was obvious that he was proud of the boy.

Thursday night, the huge double-decker car haulers were loaded. The top section was for the cars while the bottom section served as temporary living quarters and a changing area while at the track. With everything double-checked, Woody gave the signal and the Kincade Racing Team were on their way to Rockingham. It was after ten that night when they arrived at the southern entrance to the speedway. A security guard opened the gates and directed them to their garage area. Everything was unloaded and put into position so that they could begin working with the cars first thing the following morning. It was well after one in the morning by the time the team bedded down for the night. Friday would be a long day and they were going to need all the rest they could get.

Jack had expected to spend a restless night, but to his surprise he found that going to sleep was not going to be a problem. He wasn't sure if that was because of Charlie's confidence in him or a result of the confidence that the Rangers had instilled in him, but either way, he was grateful.

Work began bright and early Friday morning with Woody and his crew swarming over all three cars armed with wrenches, gauges and floor jacks. The engines were started, revved and checked inside and out. Temperatures were taken while the cars idled and when they were revved. Fuel systems and tires were checked and rechecked, along with the suspension system, transmission and rear end. It was a continuous routine that may have appeared rather monotonous to some, but one that could easily make the difference between winning and losing.

All morning the stands had been filling with race fans, while the center of the infield had become a temporary village of RVs, vans, and pick-up campers with lawn chairs of every description lining the top of each. Beer coolers and barbecue grills of every type and size were already working overtime. Saturday was going to be race day and even though this was only Friday, the good ol' boys on the infield had already laid claim to the best seats in the house.

Another reason for the appearance of the Friday crowd were the qualifying runs for Saturday's feature, which would begin at noon. Charlie was scheduled for 1:30 and Rich at 2:15. Jack had thought he would have to run a qualifier round, but was surprised to find that positions for the amateur race were made by drawing numbers. He had drawn a seventeenth place on the outside. Not the best, but better than dead last.

By Friday evening Charlie had run well enough to earn himself a number nine position on the pole and Rich had clocked well enough to work himself into the number eleven position on the outside. Immediately after the qualifying runs, Woody had both cars completely checked out again from top to bottom to assure that nothing had been affected by the time trials.

The remainder of the night was spent discussing strategy, the competition and the characteristics of the other drivers and their cars. Another check was made of the communications gear and spare equipment. Finally, just before midnight, the team went to bed with the knowledge that they had done everything possible in preparing for race day. If they weren't ready now, they never would be.

The Saturday morning sun came up as bright as ever. It was going to be a great day for racing. By noon the fans had begun to arrive and fill the stands. On the infield, smoke and the aroma of barbecue were in the air. Country music sounded from the multitude of speakers that surrounded the stadium. There was a circus atmosphere and people were having fun.

Back at the garage area, Jack was taking one more look at his car. The nervousness was beginning to build. He could feel it deep in the pit of his stomach. Looking out at the huge crowd that seemed to double in size every hour, did little to ease the nervousness. Soon he would be out there in front of that crowd. His race was scheduled to begin at 6:00 P.M. sharp.

At five o'clock Rich asked Jack to follow him to the hauler. Moving up to the living area, Rich reached into a closet and removed a bright red, white, and blue racing suit with a large black and white emblem over the pocket that read CHARLIE'S GARAGE. Jack's name appeared over the other pocket and on the back in bold black letters were the words KINCADE RACING TEAM.

"What'd you think?" asked Rich.

Jack didn't know what to say. It was the sharpest outfit he'd ever seen and it was his. "When did you guys do this? I mean, have all that work done on the shirt?"

Rich laughed, "Charlie had it done a year ago."

"A year ago!"

"Yeah, it was supposed to be a surprise for your eighteenth birthday, but we hadn't figured on meeting Judge Harting and the business with the army. You should have seen Charlie runnin' around to get a larger size after you came to the office Monday. The original would never have fit that new Ranger build of yours. Charlie hadn't figured on those rangers filling you out quite that much."

Jack reached out and took the racing suit from Rich as if it were something holy. He knew immediately that it was the most precious thing that anyone had ever given him. He was almost embarrassed as his eyes began to water up, but he fought back the tears.

"Of course, you know it's fire resistant," said Rich.

Next came the face mask, booties, and red, white and blue helmet that displayed a high-polished shine.

"Well, that's it, Jack. It's all yours. Now you get dressed. I want to take one more look at your car."

Jack thanked Rich and once he was alone in the trailer, he stared at the assortment of colorful gear that lay on the bed. For a brief moment he thought of his father and how he wished he were there to see it all. This was what his father had dreamed of doing someday. In his heart, Jack had always known that. If only he'd had the chance. Now here he stood, sensing that in a way, he was standing in the shadow of his father, preparing to fulfill his own dream. The thought gave him a warm and comforting feeling. A feeling that he was not entirely alone, nor would he be on the track.

After a few minutes, there was a tap on the door and Charlie stepped into the trailer. Jack was dressed and ready, the helmet held loosely in his hand.

"Aw, ya' look grand, Jack. How's the suit feel? Not too tight I hope?"

Again he had to fight back the tears as he smiled and replied, "It's fine, Charlie. Really fine. I can't thank you enough."

Charlie waved the thanks off. "Ya' ready?" he asked.

"Ready as I'll ever be. Let's do it."

The roar of the engines and the sound of the crowd added to the excitement Jack could feel building in his stomach. He'd thought jumping out of an airplane would be the hardest challenge he'd ever face in his life, but now he wasn't so sure. As Woody strapped him into the car, Rich and Charlie slapped his helmet for luck, then stepping back, gave him the thumbs up.

Woody adjusted the thin voice mike that he'd attached to the side of Jack's helmet.

"Give me a count, Jack."

Jack counted slowly back from five and Woody shot him a thumbs up as he said, "Loud and clear. Now Jack, you're all set. I'll be giving you a read on the positions of the other cars around you. If there's a wreck out in front of you I'll tell you to go high or low to stay clear of the mess. You just concentrate on getting to the front of the pack and holding on to the lead. You have a problem, just yell out, but be clear on exactly what the problem is. Good luck, Jack."

Woody backed away from the car. The time for talking was over. The low rumble of the big Chevy engine sent the blood throbbing through Jack's veins. He shifted down and moved the car out onto the track and began to merge with the slow circling pack. One by one they began to drop into their designated positions until they became one single mass of metal and rubber moving as one unit around the track.

Coming out of the third turn, Jack's eyes were on the flagman leaning out from the catwalk at the starting line. Woody had told him not to worry about the flag, he'd let him know if and when it was a start, but Jack seemed mesmerized by the man holding the green flag. It all suddenly seemed so unreal—more like a dream, but the smell of fuel and hot metal assured him that it was no dream.

Coming down the straightaway, the flagman held the green flag high above his head, checking the alignment of the pack and the positioning of the cars. Satisfied that all was in order and they had a good line-up, the starter suddenly brought the flag down and began waving it wildly. The race was on.

Woody's voice suddenly boomed in Jack's ear. "Green! Green! Go! Go! Go Jack! Push it to the outside!"

Jack floored the Chevy and shot to the outside, shifting as he swung high only inches from the wall and pushed the Chevy for all she was worth. In a matter of seconds, he had leaped from seventeenth position to thirteenth, and they hadn't even completed the first lap yet.

The adrenaline was pumping and his heart was pounding as they went into the first turn with only inches separating the cars. Opening it up again on the straightaway, Jack was pegging at nearly 115 miles an hour. He thought that was fast until he heard Woody's voice again, booming, "Come on, Jack! Don't baby the damn thing—get on it, son. Get on it!"

Backing off to go into the curve, Jack's heart nearly stopped as he felt a car tap his right-rear bumper and the Chevy slid ever so slightly to the left. Charlie had preached at him that the only way to keep from getting those kind of little love taps was to get out front, take the

lead, and stay there. That was exactly what Jack intended
to do when they came out of the next turn.

"Woody, how many cars in front of me?" he asked.

"Twelve," came the reply.

"I'm going to make a jailbreak on the next straightaway, Woody. Keep an eye out for me."

Woody's voice was suddenly calm as he answered,
"You're the man, Jack. Go for it."

They came out of the curve at 105 miles an hour,
everyone scrambling to go low—everyone that is except
Jack, who swung out and went to the high side of the
track, his accelerator planted firmly to the floor.

The speedometer and tach jumped in a matter of seconds. One hundred fifteen, 125, 130 miles per hour. Jack
was flying high as he blew past eight cars as if they were
standing still. Then came the unexpected. The fifth-place
car, seeing Jack's rapid approach, decided that he would
go high as well before the next turn. Unfortunately, the
number four car had the same idea and they made the
move at the same time. In the blink of an eye their
bumpers collided and they both went into sideways skids.
Burning rubber and smoke practically obscured the two
cars as they began to spin a full 360 degrees and went
into the wall with an ear-splitting crash that sent fenders,
tires and bumpers catapulting into the middle of the
track.

"Go low, Jack! Go low!" screamed Woody through
the headset.

Jack backed the Chevy off and cut the wheel to the left
to miss the flying debris. A tire bounced off his right
fender and went careening into the infield. At the same
moment, the car directly behind him glanced off of his
rear bumper and went into a spin that drove two other
cars into the wall.

"Get in the middle, Jack! The middle! We got yellow

all over the place. Back off your speed and bring her in on the next pass. We'll check you out for damage."

Jack swung into pit row on the next pass and brought the Chevy to the stop line directly in front of the pit crew. Someone pushed a water bottle at him through the driver's side window. He needed it. His mouth felt as dry as Death Valley. Taking a long drink, he lowered the bottle and suddenly realized that his hand was shaking. Charlie was at the side window and noticed the bottle. He winked, then smiled, as he said, "Don't let it bother ya, son. You're doin' just fine out there. Only forty-five more laps to go. Hang in there."

Jesus, thought Jack. Five laps—that's all we've done. It already felt like a hundred. There was a sudden bounce as the screw jack on the driver's side was released, dropping the car. "Get out of here, Jack!" shouted Charlie. "You're number six in the line-up."

Over the next thirty laps there were three more crashes that took out six more cars. Jack had taken the opportunity during one of the caution flags to pit for two new tires and gas. The final crash found him holding on to seventh place, with fourteen laps remaining in the race. As the cars regrouped for another start, Jack's excitement was still running high; his only thought—fourteen more laps. Fourteen more times around the big circle!

Once again the green flag was dropped and the Chevy accelerator went to the floor. One hundred ten, 125, 130 miles an hour, faster and faster. Downshifting on the curves, accelerating on the straightaway. Ten laps to go and Jack had moved up to fifth place. For a fleeting moment he thought he saw a chance to shoot the gap low and sweep the number four car, but just as he started to make the move, Woody warned him off. "No, Jack! Back off! He's baiting you. Stay back."

No sooner had Woody's warning come over the headset, than the number four car swept low into the slot. If

Jack had made his move, he would have been pushed to the edge of the infield and at these speeds, it was a good bet he would have spun out, or worse.

"Thanks, Woody," whispered Jack into the mike.

"Hey, that's what I'm here for. Hang close until turn three, Jack. That boy has a tendency to swing out a little too high on that turn. We'll get him there. Be ready."

Jack stayed right on the number-four car's bumper as they neared the third turn. Sure enough, just as Woody had said, the driver went into the curve deep, but then casually began to drift high as they prepared to come out of the curve.

"Now, Jack!" shouted Woody. "Hit the slot and punch it!"

Jack swung down into the slot, accelerating rather than backing off, and shot the gap before the number-four car could dive down to cut him off. Jack was now in fourth place and wasn't about to give it up. The way he saw it, there were eight laps left to go and three cars in front of him. Fourth place wasn't bad, but first was a hell of a lot better.

By the forty-fourth lap, Jack realized that the three drivers in front of him were not going to make any mistakes. He had already tried to bait the third-place car, but the driver wasn't going for it. He had even tried to outrun him on the straightaway, but as good as the Chevy was running, the number-three Dodge was running even better.

When the race had gone down to only three laps left to go, Jack had made one more attempt at matching horsepower with the Dodge. While the Chevy was maxed out, they were running side by side, but the extra punch that Jack needed just wasn't there. The next voice he'd heard over the radio was Charlie. "Back it off, Jack. Nothing wrong with a fourth-place finish your first time out. Back off and take the sure thing, son. Ya copy?"

"Roger, loud and clear."

The final two laps were anti-climactic for Jack, who did as instructed and simply rode out the final two laps, securing a fourth-place finish and a check for $850.

Rolling the car to a stop at the garage area, he was amazed to discover how stiff he suddenly felt as he climbed from the Chevy. It was a sign of the tension and the stress experienced with each and every lap, as well as the constant movement of clutching and shifting through the turns.

He may have only finished fourth, but you'd never have guessed that by the greeting he received as he exited the car. A loud and thunderous cheer rose from the crowd around him, followed by a wave of handshaking and back-slapping. But no one could have been as proud as Charlie and Rich. They had just served notice that another Kincade had arrived on the scene and they were going to have a hell of a time dealing with him.

The feature race didn't turn out as well for Rich and Charlie. Rich could only manage to finish twenty-third, while Charlie finished next to last. But on the drive home that night, none of that seemed to matter. The entire conversation revolved around Jack and how well he had performed in his first big race. A race that they knew was only the first of many that would follow.

12

Between his duties at Fort Bragg and what seemed like never-ending training exercises, Jack still managed to find the time to run in two more amateur races before the season was over, finishing third at Charlotte and second at Darlington. Charlie swore that if the boy could spend a complete summer on the circuit he had a damn good chance of winning the whole thing—he was that good. But any plans for that kind of run would have to wait. Right after New Year's Day, 1989, Jack's detachment received orders assigning them to Panama for six months. That, in effect, wiped out any chance for racing that summer. Jack was disappointed, but then, this was his job. It was what he had trained so hard for all those months. He was a Ranger and Rangers went anywhere, anytime, without question.

During the summer of '89, Rich and Charlie wrote him often, keeping him up to date on what was happening on the circuit with news of who was winning, what they were driving and how the money was getting bigger all the time in the racing game. Charlie felt that if they could just stay in the top twenty of the points standings until the end of the season, they might actually show a profit. That would be a first in over twenty years.

Rich's letters talked about pretty much the same things except for when he wrote about Charlie. There was little doubt in his mind now that Charlie had something major wrong with him. They had run a race in Winston-Salem at the start of the season. Midway through the qualifying rounds, Rich had gone to the trailer to find out what was holding Charlie up. His qualifying run was coming up in a few minutes and he hadn't even made it to his car yet.

Once inside the trailer, Rich found his brother bent over in pain, a bottle of pain-killers lying just out of reach. There was blood on a towel next to the bed. Charlie had used it to wipe his mouth after a violent coughing spell. Rich had started to go for a doctor, but Charlie stopped him. He had Rich give him the pills and a glass of water. Ten minutes later, he swore he was feeling fine and went straight to his car. His qualifying time was one of the best he'd had so far that year and he finished the race with a fifth-place showing.

Rich had made him promise he'd see a doctor when they got back home, but of course, Charlie blew it off as soon as they got back. He still hadn't seen a doctor and the supply of pills was getting larger. Although Rich told him not to worry, he'd see to it that Charlie got to a doctor one way or another. Jack had a bad feeling that it was already too late for that. Rich wasn't saying it in his letter, but Jack knew they were both thinking the same thing . . . Charlie had cancer.

Two months later, Jack received another letter from Rich. Charlie's health had gotten so bad that he no longer could drive and he still hadn't seen a doctor. Woody Clark had volunteered to drive Charlie's car till the end of the season, but Woody had proved to be a better pit boss than a race car driver. His first time out at the Charlotte Speedway he totaled Charlie's car out on the tenth lap. He wasn't hurt, but the experience of colliding with a wall at 135 miles an hour had convinced the top mechanic that he should stay with what he knew best— fixing them, not racing them.

Charlie had been so disgusted that he wasn't even going to rebuild the car. Since the '88 season was almost over anyway, he didn't see any sense in it. For the first time in ten years, a Kincade car had not finished in the top twenty of the points standings. Rich had closed his letter with the words, "Wish you were here."

With the letter still on his mind, Jack headed into the town of Colón and for his favorite bar. He found a table in a secluded corner and ordered a beer. As he waited for his drink, his thoughts kept going back to Charlie and his memories of the scrapping, big-fisted man that he had known all his life. It didn't seem possible that anything, even cancer, could bring down that tough old man. He was only in his late fifties—that wasn't old. Jack fought to push the thought of him dying out of his mind. Maybe there was still time if they got him into a good hospital. Maybe it wasn't too late.

The waitress returned with his beer and asked if he would like some company, pointing to three Panamanian girls at the bar. Jack waved off the invitation. He wasn't in the mood for company at the moment. The waitress shrugged her shoulders, "Okay. You change your mind, you let me know, okay? I fix you up."

"Sure," said Jack, as he took a long drink from the bottle of beer, then set it on the table and stared at it for a long minute. Even the beer wasn't going to help change what he already knew—Charlie wasn't going to make it.

He was on his fifth beer and still just as depressed as he had been when he arrived, when he heard a familiar voice behind him saying, "Playing the lone wolf tonight, are we?"

Jack's face instantly brightened as he turned in his chair and saw Deke approaching with that long Texas stride of his. Jumping to his feet, Jack grabbed the big man. "Jesus Christ, they let anybody into this damn country—even redheaded shits from Texas."

The old friends wrestled around a bit then, waving for more beer, sat down at the table.

"Damn, Deke. What are you doing in Panama? You get caught checking out the wrong set of hooters or what?"

Deke grinned, "Aw, no, nothing like that, Jack. They say they brought us down here for some kind of extensive training exercise. We just got in yesterday. They gave us the night off."

Seeing Deke again was just the medicine Jack needed to snap him out of his depression.

"You seen or heard from Tyrell lately?" asked Deke.

"Yeah, he came to Charlotte and spent a weekend with me before I left to come down here. He's looking great and doing pretty well. They've already made him a buck sergeant at the school."

"No, shit. I'm suppose to make sergeant when we get back. Or so they say. You should be gettin' pretty close to promotion yourself shouldn't you, Jack?"

Jack smiled, "Yeah, get my stripes in a couple of days. Just about everybody that came down with us is getting promoted. What kind of exercise you guys runnin' down here, Deke?"

Deke's expression suddenly turned serious. He leaned forward and in almost a whisper said, "Between you and me, I don't think there *is* an exercise."

Jack looked confused for a moment, then asked, "What the hell you talking about, Deke?"

Deke tapped Jack's hand, "Not so loud, man."

Looking around to make sure no one was close enough to hear, Deke continued in a low voice. "Something is up, Jack. I'm not a hundred percent certain what or where, but trust me, whatever they flew us in here for wasn't some rinky-dink training exercise. We're carrying too much of the classified shit with us—special weapons, the works. Stuff we only break out for the real thing, ya' know what I mean."

Jack nodded that he understood, then quietly said, "We've been having a rough time down here with old pineapple face. Noriega's special police have been harassing Americans, both military and civilian. Could be President Bush has had enough of his crap."

"That was the first thing I thought, too," said Deke. "But I'm not so sure anymore." Leaning closer, he whispered, "We picked up four guys in civilian clothes and those super-spook sunglasses when we landed in Florida. Now I may be just a dumb ol' Texas boy, but I'd bet my horse that them boys were DEA or CIA."

Jack was getting a little confused by now. If Deke was right, then that would fit in with the trouble they were having with Manuel Noriega, and Jack said so. But Deke only shook his head. "I don't think so, Jack. Master Sergeant Turner is our intell man for the unit and another good ol' Texas boy. Well, anyway, he was gathering up a shitload of maps and intell reports on Colombia."

"How do you know all this, Deke?" asked Jack.

"Me and a couple of other guys were helping him load the stuff on the bird for the trip down here when one of the footlockers got knocked off the stack. It hit the tarmac hard enough to break it open and all this Colombia shit fell out. Man, I thought Turner was going to have a heart attack right there. He made everybody clear the area until he got it repacked, but it was Colombia, all right. I'm sure of that. You guys heard anything about trouble down that way?"

"No, nothing. Only the Noriega problem," said Jack.

Deke sat back in his chair and sipped on his beer for a minute. Maybe he was all wrong. Maybe it was all just the result of an overactive imagination, or just wishful thinking on his part that they were going to get a real live mission for a change. But either way, he knew what he saw lying on that runway. And the weapons they'd brought along were never used except in a real-world situation. So why'd they have them along? And just who the hell were the four suits that had joined them in Florida? Now even Deke was getting confused by it all. Each question only begot another question. So many, in fact, that Deke put the matter aside and asked about Charlie and Rich.

Jack told him the bad news about Charlie and the hard luck they were having on the circuit this season. The sadness felt by Deke on hearing the news about Charlie was clearly visible in his young face. He liked the brothers, especially Charlie. He'd never forget that pair of binoculars with the tag Charlie had left atop Woody Clark's RV at that first race. It was those types of memories that made Deke tell the waitress to start bringing the beer, four bottles at a time. If he was going to feel depressed, he might as well be drunk, too.

The beer and the talk went on well past midnight, with Jack finally calling an end to it. He paid the bar tab then helped Deke outside. Propping him up against the wall, he hailed a cab and told the driver to head for the base. Deke immediately went to sleep on the ride back. Jack chalked that up to the booze and jet lag. But that was all right. His thoughts were occupied with other things—primarily, a place called Colombia.

13

The following morning began as any other normal day. P.T. at 0530 hours. A workout, then a five-mile run. Showers and then breakfast at the mess hall, with a company formation in front of the barracks at 0800. But from that moment on, nothing was going to seem normal to Jack again.

The commander, Captain Marcus, called the group to attention, then said, "The following personnel will report to the operations center immediately following this formation: Allen, Curry, Dolan, Felps, Henderson, Jacobs, Kincade, Morton, and Sanders. The rest of you report to the arms room and draw your weapons—we're at the range today. That's it. Company dismissed."

Jack and the eight other Rangers double-timed to the operations center. No one had any idea what was going on or why they had been selected and no one asked. They'd know soon enough. The sergeant major was waiting for them as they came down the hallway that led to the Op Center. He was normally a jovial sort of fellow who could bite your head off the second you screwed up,

but you got the sense that he was only doing it because
that was what sergeant majors were supposed to do. But
there was nothing jovial about the look on his face at the
moment. He was all business and it showed.

"Okay, rangers," he said, "get in there and find yourself a seat and keep your mouth shut unless someone asks
you a question. Are we clear?"

The words, "Yes, Sergeant Major," were spoken in
unison.

The men filed into the room and around a huge table
that sat before a map of Central and South America. As
Jack moved to an open seat near the end of the table, he
saw Deke sitting on the other side. The Texan winked at
him as he sat down. Before Jack could even get comfortable in the chair, a full-bird colonel walked into the room
followed by a one-star general. The colonel yelled,
"Attention!" Everyone rose quickly to their feet. The
general walked to the end of the table as he said, "Be
seated, gentlemen."

The colonel moved behind the senior officer and
reaching up, pulled down a map of Colombia. Jack
glanced over at Deke, who smiled and winked again.
He'd been right all along.

"Gentlemen, my name is General Gates. I serve as the
liaison for Special Operations at the Pentagon. In the past
seventy-two hours we have had a situation develop
involving thirty-nine American civilian citizens. At
approximately 0220 hours Thursday morning, a well-
armed force of anti-government guerrillas attacked the
Americana Hotel in the Colombia city of Villavicencio
located one hundred miles southeast of Bogota. They
killed nineteen people in the attack, mostly hotel staff
personnel, and conducted a systematic search of the
rooms seeking out Americans to be held as hostages. The
local police and paramilitary units of the city either
lacked the time to get organized or simply chose to with-

draw rather than face a confrontation with the guerrillas. It is not exactly clear why no action was taken, although a number of us have our own opinions on that matter, which I will not state here.

"The rangers in this room, working in conjunction with members of the Seventh Special Forces Group, will be flown to Villavicencio this evening. Once there you will conduct operations to eliminate the guerrillas and recover the hostages. Satellite intelligence on the area is being gathered as we speak.

"Gentlemen, I cannot emphasize enough the importance of this operation. There are a number of high-ranking officials and V.I.P. personnel among the hostages. It is imperative that we bring them home safe and sound. I have no doubt that you men in this room are more than capable of doing just that. I wish you good luck and God-speed."

The general turned to leave. Every man automatically rose to his feet. Not a word was spoken until the general had left the room. He had done his part. Next, the colonel went through a list of what equipment was to be taken. Time schedules and modes of transportation. Types of aircraft to be used and what actions were to be taken once they landed. He ended the briefing with a resounding, "Airborne Ranger! All the way!"

In a matter of hours Deke and Jack were sitting side by side on a C-130 aircraft bound for Bogota, Colombia. It certainly was a far cry from North Carolina or Texas. For Jack, all thoughts of home were put aside. There was nothing now but the mission and the desire to remove thirty-nine American citizens from harm's way.

"You scared, Deke?" asked Jack.

"Damn straight, brother. Man's a damn fool if he ain't."

Jack agreed. His stomach had been twisted in knots ever since they had boarded the aircraft. He was grateful for the fact that Deke was there. It made him feel more at ease with his own fear.

It was nighttime when the plane touched down in Bogota and taxied to a specially designated area to be unloaded. As the rear ramp came down, the rangers were greeted by a detachment of Special Forces Green Berets and escorted to six helicopters that were already cranking up for takeoff. Within twenty minutes the lights of Bogota were fading in the distance. Jack was just beginning to enjoy the warm night air rushing through the open doors of the choppers, when one of the green beret sergeants tapped Captain Marcus on the shoulder and pointed out lights in the distance. It was Villavicencio.

The choppers banked one after the other as they came into a landing zone that had already been secured by another green beret team. The LZ was located about three miles from the outskirts of the town, in a small valley. As the choppers touched down, the rangers scrambled out the doors and ran for the surrounding woods, dropping to the ground once they were in the treeline. Deke and his team were just to the right of Jack. He could barely make them out in the darkness. As the last chopper lifted off, the sound of its rotor blades faded and there was suddenly nothing but perfect silence.

Ten minutes . . . fifteen minutes, Jack wasn't sure how long they lay there. All he could hear was his heart pounding a mile a minute. Then he suddenly grinned to himself—and he had thought driving his first race was a hell of an experience!

Quietly, the word was passed to move out. An advanced special forces team had located the guerrilla base camp. Two of the green berets had come back to lead the rangers into position. It almost seemed impossible to Jack that thirty men were moving through the trees; there wasn't a sound that could be heard coming from anywhere, yet, they were all moving at a steady pace. He estimated they had gone no more than two miles before he saw the faint glow of a small fire in the distance. The general had been right. It didn't appear that the local authorities were in any hurry for a confrontation with the guerrillas. This base camp couldn't be more than three or four miles from the outskirts of the town itself.

Everyone stopped and went down. From here they would slowly work their way toward the camp, spreading out to silently form a circle. Slowly, quietly, Jack inched his way forward. The adrenalin had kicked in and he could feel the sweat in the palms of his hands. Reaching forward, he suddenly jerked his hand back. He had touched something—it felt like an arm and a shirt, but it hadn't moved. Crawling forward again, he found himself face to face with one of the guerrillas. His eyes were wide open, staring up at the night stars. His throat had been cut from ear to ear. The SF boys had taken out the sentries.

Inching his way around the body, Jack kept moving forward until he felt Captain Marcus, who was on his right, tap his shoulder and signal for him to stop. They were close enough now for Jack to hear voices. They were speaking in Spanish. Jack heard the captain cuss under his breath. "What is it, sir?" he whispered.

Marcus quietly said, "They moved five of the hostages to a coffee warehouse just this side of the town."

The captain wasn't the only one that had overheard the conversation. An SF sergeant suddenly appeared at his side and whispered, "Sir, we can't take these guys out without risking the loss of those five people at that warehouse."

"I know," said Marcus. "The minute they hear the firing, they'll kill those people for sure."

The sergeant agreed. "Give me four of your men and one hour to locate that warehouse. At exactly twenty-three-hundred hours you take these guys down. Hope-

fully, we'll have located the other five by then. If not . . .
at least we tried."

"Okay," said Marcus. "Twenty-three hundred hours it
is. Kincade, you, Sanders, Felps and Jacobs go with the
sergeant."

"Yes, Sir," whispered Jack, as he and the other three
rangers slipped off into the darkness with the SF trooper.

Suddenly, time had become a factor as the men made
their way through the trees for the lights on the outskirts
of the town. They were almost running, any thought of
moving quietly forgotten. They were on the clock and so
were the lives of five innocent Americans.

Stopping at the treeline, the group found themselves
on the edge of town. Three large tin buildings were sil-
houetted by the city lights. From the information the
sergeant had obtained in earlier intell reports, one of
those buildings had to be the coffee warehouse—but
which one?

They would have to split up. The sergeant took the
one in the center. Jack and Sanders would take the one on
the left, and Jacobs and Felps the one on the right. The SF
sergeant gave each ranger a small transmitter. "Okay,
these are light signal only. You can't talk with them. I'm
one; Felps, you're two; and Kincade, you're three. If you
find our warehouse, signal and the rest of us will con-
verge on your position. Any questions? Good. Remember, no firing unless it's absolutely necessary. Let's go."

Jack and Hank Sanders moved toward their target,
using the shadows for cover. Coming to one corner of the
warehouse, Jack could see movement through one of the
windows, but the glass was so dirty he couldn't tell if it
was a man or a woman. "There's somebody in there," he
whispered to Sanders.

"Guerrilla or hostage?" asked Hank.

"Can't tell," said Jack. Wetting his fingers, he slowly
rubbed a small area on the pane of glass until it was clean

enough to see through. Moving closer to the window, he stared through the small spot. His heart skipped a beat when he saw a man with a beard and combat fatigues, carrying a Russian AK-47. This had to be one of the guerrillas. Jack tried to locate any sign of the hostages, but his range of vision was limited through the small hole. He was about to give up, when suddenly, another well-armed guerrilla came out of a small room located directly across from the window. There they were. Four men and a young woman. Their hands were tied behind their backs and they were sitting in a row of chairs against the wall.

"Got 'em!" whispered Jack. "Send the signal."

In a matter of minutes, the sergeant, Felps and Jacobs came around the corner to join them. "What'd you got?" asked the SF NCO.

"Five hostages—four male, one female. Small room north side of the warehouse. No visible windows to the room. Hands tied behind their backs. They're in chairs, but I don't think they're tied to them. Visual on two bad guys—carryin' AK's. Could be more. I don't know."

The sergeant nodded, obviously impressed with Jack's attention to detail in the situation report. Pulling a 9mm Beretta from his shoulder holster, the sergeant twisted a silencer into place, then glanced at his watch. "Twenty-two-forty-five hours. We've got fifteen minutes before the party starts. Kincade, you and Sanders are on me. Felps, you and Jacobs take the back door, we'll go in the front. Once you're in, watch your firing, but don't let anyone get to that room before us. They'll kill those people if they can. We ready?"

Everyone nodded silently. "Let's get in position, then."

For Jack, that fifteen-minute wait was the longest of his life. Then suddenly, off in the direction of the guerrilla camp, the rattle of automatic weapons fire and explosions shattered the silence. The sergeant kicked open the door and leaped into the room, startling the two guerrillas that had already started across the warehouse to kill the hostages. As they both turned to the door, the SF sergeant fired, killing one instantly, but before he could get a shot at the second one, he was hit by a burst of rifle fire. Jack squeezed off three rapid rounds from his rifle before he realized it. All three hit the guerrilla dead center in the chest, dropping the man like a load of rocks to the floor. He was dead.

Jack had just killed a man, but he didn't have time to think about that now. He rushed to the small room, while Sanders covered the front. Kicking the door open, Jack quickly swept the room with his rifle for any other possible targets. But the hostages were the only ones in the room. Their faces had gone from expressions of pure terror to one of sudden relief at seeing the American flag insignia and the ranger tab on the shoulder of Jack's uniform. Pulling his knife from his web gear, Jack cut the first man free then gave him the knife to free the others, while he went back to the door to keep watch.

Now that they had the hostages, what were they supposed to do with them? The sergeant was dead and Jack couldn't see taking them back toward the guerrilla camp. The risk was too high that they would run into guerrillas fleeing the battle. But what was he to do with them? He was still pondering that question when Sanders suddenly jumped back from the front door and yelled, "Oh Shit, Jack! There's two jeeps loaded with guerrillas coming this way! What do we do?"

"How many?" shouted Jack.

"Twelve . . . maybe more. Too damn many for us!"

The sounds of gunfire erupted from the rear of the warehouse. It was a firefight and Felps and Jacobs were smack in the middle of it. Jack turned to the hostages. The young girl was shaking. A gray-haired man in his mid-sixties held her, trying to comfort her. Jack guessed that the man was her father—and he was right.

"Better make a decision quick, Jack. They'll be at the front door in a few minutes," yelled Sanders.

Jack suddenly found himself in charge and everyone waiting for him to call the shots.

"Hank! Toss a few grenades their way. We're buggin' out the back. We'll take our chances in the open."

Sanders grabbed three grenades, pulled the pins, then tossed them out in front of the warehouse and ran for the back to join the others. Jack was rounding up the hostages. "Come on, folks. We've gotta' move and right now!"

With Jack in the lead and Sanders covering their backs, the group ran outside. Jack wasn't prepared for the sight that greeted them. Jacobs and Felps lay side by side, covered in blood. They were obviously dead. The bodies of eight dead guerrillas littered the ground around the two rangers. They hadn't died without extracting a heavy price from the enemy.

In the distance they could still hear gunfire coming from the guerrilla camp. At the same instant, Sanders's grenades exploded at the front door. "Come on! Follow me," yelled Jack, as he led the group down a poorly lit street and into an alleyway. For the moment they were safe. If they were lucky, the grenades had done the job on the troops in the jeeps. But they weren't that lucky. Within seconds, the two jeeps came tearing around the corner of the warehouse and the street. Jack got everyone back into the shadows just as the vehicles shot past the alley.

"They didn't see us," said one of the hostages.

"Yeah—this time. But it won't take them long to figure out they missed us. They'll be back. We've got to keep moving."

"Where in the hell are the police? The army? No one

in this town is doing anything to help us," said one of the men. The man with the daughter answered, "That's because they've either been paid off or are too scared to tangle with these guys."

Jack led them down another street and into another alley. He had no idea where they were or where they were going, but at least they were still alive. The sound of the jeeps racing up and down the streets was beginning to close in on them. Jack knew they couldn't play this cat and mouse game much longer. They knew the town—he didn't. It was just a matter of time before he led them down a wrong street or around the wrong corner and into a hail of rifle fire.

Pausing in an archway to allow them to catch their breath, Jack was beginning to experience a hint of self-doubt, a slipping away of his confidence. Just then, he felt a hand on his shoulder. It was the man with the daughter. They were both staring at him as the man asked, "What's your name, son?"

"Kincade . . . Specialist Jack Kincade, Sir."

Squeezing the shoulder slightly, the man smiled as he said, "My name is Ross Ward and this is my daughter, Karen. We just wanted to say thanks, and tell you that you're doing a fine job, Jack."

Jack was almost embarrassed. "Thank you, Sir. But we haven't got you all out of here, yet."

Mr. Ward grinned, "That's so, son. But by God, at least we're a lot closer than we were a couple of hours ago."

The man's sense of humor and pleasing tone instantly put Jack at ease, making him more determined than ever to get these people out alive.

The group continued their game of hide-and-seek for another three blocks, finally coming upon an unlocked door that led into a small warehouse. Jack led the group inside. There were a number of crates stacked in the center of the floor marked COFFEE. In one of the corners, a few old desks and chairs were stacked against the wall. Across the room was what appeared to be a large object covered by a tarp. While Sanders kept watch at the door, and the others rested, Jack crossed the room to take a closer look at the tarp. Mr. Ward joined him.

"What is that, Jack?" he asked.

"No idea," said the ranger, as he grabbed a corner of the tarp and slowly raised it up.

"Well, I'll be damned," said Ross Ward. "I haven't seen one of those in that condition for years."

"I have," said Jack, as he pulled the tarp off to reveal a coal black 1964 Chevy Impala that appeared to be straight off the assembly line. It was a thing of beauty.

"Do you think it still runs?" asked Ward.

"We're going to find out," replied Jack, handing his rifle to Ward.

With Sanders still at the door, the others gathered around the car while Jack searched around inside for any sign of the keys. He was about to give up when Karen Ward reached inside the car and flipped the visor down. The keys dropped like magic into Jack's lap. "Thanks," he said with a smile.

"Don't mention it," she replied with a grin that almost made Jack forget why he was there.

Placing the key in the ignition, he crossed his fingers and turned. The big V-8 engine instantly roared to life. It was the sweetest sound Jack had ever heard, and it came with a bonus—the gas tank was full.

Yelling to Sanders to open the double doors, Jack told everyone to get in the car. It was going to be a little crowded, but nobody was complaining. It beat walking. Jack checked his watch as Sanders was squeezing his way into the car. It was 2340 hours. He found it hard to believe that only forty minutes had passed since the attack had begun, but he had heard firing coming from the guerrilla camp when they had been running down the street. That had been twenty minutes ago. Jack was now trying to figure time and distance. It would take the attack team five minutes or so to get the hostages rounded up; another twenty to thirty minutes to move them to the landing zone for extraction. The chopper would already be on-site; another five minutes to load everyone. The way he figured it, his small group had, at the outside, maybe fifteen minutes to get out of this town and back to the LZ. Hank had been doing some figuring of his own as he said, "We'll be cuttin' it pretty damn close, Jack. An' you know those choppers won't wait."

"Yeah, I know, Hank. But you've obviously never rode with a tripper."

"With a what?" asked Sanders.

"A moonshiner," said Mr. Ward from the back seat.

Hank Sanders looked at the young man from North Carolina and shook his head. "Well, I'll be damned. Okay, Jack—show us your best stuff."

Jack's answer came in the form of squealing tires and a cloud of smoke as he barreled the Chevy through the open double doors and onto the streets of Villavicencio.

"Which way back to the warehouse?" shouted Jack, to no one in particular.

One of the men in the back who was more familiar with the town told him to go two blocks west, then north for three more.

Jack had just made the turn back north when one of the jeeps, loaded with guerrillas, came out of an alleyway behind them. Spotting the car and the people inside, they swung the jeep around and began chasing the Chevy down the street. Jack yelled for everyone to hang on, then floored the big V-8. The narrow streets made maneuvering at high speeds more than a little hazardous. Everyone in the car was looking a little pale, all except for Ross Ward, who actually seemed to be enjoying the wild ride.

Coming to a corner, Jack hit the brake, cut left and hit the gas all in the same motion, taking the corner sideways, then whipping the car back right before roaring off, up the middle of the street. In his mirror, Jack watched the jeep miss the turn and tip over on its side, spilling guerrillas all over the street.

"You've got to go right here!"

Jack geared down and made the turn. The warehouse suddenly appeared on the right. A group of armed men were gathered around a jeep in front of the building.

"Guerrillas, Jack!" shouted Sanders.

"Can't be helped! We gotta' go through 'em. Everybody stay low."

Kicking the Chevy accelerator to the floor, Jack headed straight for the group of men. Before they knew what was happening, the car was closing in on them. Screaming and yelling they went diving in all directions as Jack narrowly missed the jeep. He swung the Chevy off the road, cutting across a field, through a make-shift fence, then headed for the treeline, leaving the rattle of rifle fire behind them. Hank looked over the dash.

"I don't see the road, Jack!"

"That's because there isn't one. If we're going to make that LZ in time, it's going to have to be done using straight-line distance. Hold on, everybody. This could turn into a rough ride."

Dodging trees, jumping ditches and bottoming out every now and then, Jack drove the Chevy as if it were a battle tank, all the time hoping and praying that he was going in the right direction. Suddenly, any doubt he may have had was gone when he caught the outline of a chopper rising along the horizon. But what if that was the last one out? Jack began flashing his lights and honking his horn. He hadn't taken these people through all this just to end up being left in the middle of an LZ with no way home.

Bringing the car to a sliding, sideways stop in the middle of a field, Jack ordered everyone out just as a swarm of rangers surrounded them. Captain Marcus came running up to Jack.

"Damn, Kincade! We figured you guys had bought it."

Jack wiped the sweat from his forehead as he answered, "The SF Sarge, Felps and Jacobs did, sir. We didn't have time to recover the bodies . . . figured the hostages were the first priority."

Marcus nodded his approval. "Good decision, Ranger. Some of you men get these people on those choppers. Kincade, you and Sanders go with them." Turning to his executive officer, Marcus continued, "Keep two choppers here. We're going in to recover the bodies."

Jack suddenly stepped forward. "Captain Marcus, Sir. I'd like to go with you."

"No, Sergeant Kincade—and it will be Sergeant, just as soon as we get back. You've already done your part and done it well, Ranger. We can handle this. See you back in Bogota."

Reluctantly, Jack and Sanders boarded a chopper and were on their way back to Bogota by the time Captain Marcus had reached the outskirts of town. The guerrillas had apparently had enough and decided to cut their losses and run. The body recovery was made without a shot being fired. By morning, the entire unit, including the dead, were being loaded on a C-130 aircraft for the trip home to Panama. Supervising some of the loading near the rear ramp, Jack looked up and saw Deke coming across the tarmac. He had a bloodstained bandage tied to the side of his face. Deke could see the worried look in Jack's face as he neared the ramp.

"Awh, don't worry about it, Jack. They got a mite close, but no cigar. I hear you been racing again. What'd they call it? Oh, yeah! The Villavicencio 500."

Jack simply shook his head. Grinning, he asked, "Deke, do you ever take anything serious?"

"Hell, no! Life's too short to be worrying about serious shit. Hey, man. You get a peek at any hooters in that place?"

Captain Marcus walked up while the two rangers were still laughing. "Kincade, Mister Ward and his daughter would like to speak to you a minute. Go ahead. I won't let the plane leave without you."

Jack jogged across the runway to the operations shack. Ward and his daughter were waiting for him near the gate. Ross Ward reached out and grasped Jack's hand. "Just wanted to thank you again, Jack, for everything you did for us."

Jack was almost embarrassed. "It wasn't just me, sir."

Ward still held a firm grip on Jack's hand as he said, "Oh, I know that, Jack. But you were the one that took charge when things started going bad out there. I believe they would have killed us all if it hadn't been for you."

"Daddy's right you know," said Karen. "You're the one that made the difference, Jack." Leaning forward, she kissed him on the cheek. "Thank you."

Her father reached into his coat pocket, withdrew a card and passed it on to Jack. It was his business card. He then asked, "One thing I'd like to know, Jack."

"Yes, sir."

"The way you handled that car . . . well, were you really a tripper?"

Jack half-smiled. He really was embarrassed now. "Yes, sir. Made the run only once and got caught. That was the end of that career, I can assure you."

Ward laughed. "Well, you sure as hell can drive a car, son. You keep that card I just gave you. If there's ever anything I can do for you, just give me a call. Or better yet, come on down to Dallas. We always got room at the ranch for heroes. I mean it, Jack. You need anything. You let me know. We owe you, son."

Jack took a fleeting glance at the card and put it in his pocket. "Really, sir. That's not necessary. I was just doing my job. But thank you for the kind offer."

Ward nodded, slapped the boy on the shoulder and said good-bye, then walked to the operations shack. Karen lingered a moment, but before she left, she said, "I hope you will come to Dallas, Jack. I really do. Good-bye."

Jack was still thinking of Karen's smile as he walked back to the plane. Deke was waiting for him. "Okay Jack. Just what was that all about? I didn't have any hostages with great hooters kissin' around on me."

Jack explained what had happened at the warehouse, then removed the business card from his pocket and handed it to Deke. The Texan stared at the card for a moment then muttered, "Holy shit, Jack. Don't you know who that guy is?"

"Yeah. A nice guy with a great-looking daughter."

Deke almost staggered back as he said, "Some guy! Jesus, Jack! That so-called guy as you call him just happens to be one of the richest men in Texas—hell, probably one of the richest in the world. Just about every kind of gas or oil you put in a motor comes from one of his refineries. He's the only guy I know that could match checkbooks with NASA . . . and his daughter just planted a kiss on you . . . holy shit, man."

Jack was more than surprised by the news. He'd been around people with big money before. Nearly all of them had been stuck-up snobs, or regular assholes, but Ross Ward wasn't at all like that. And Karen certainly wasn't the typical spoiled little rich girl. But it really didn't matter. As nice as they were, Jack knew they were totally out of his class. Still, he knew he wouldn't soon forget them.

14

By the summer of 1989, Jack had his new rank and was quickly getting the reputation among the group as a young man on the rise who could get things done. And with tensions between the Americans and the Noriega faction quickly deteriorating, everyone knew it was only a matter of time before the war of words would escalate into a war of guns and bullets. But it was a war that would have to be fought without Jack Kincade.

Charlie was dying. Jack's mother, working through the Red Cross, had requested that Jack be reassigned to Fort Bragg. Charlie had practically raised the boy and it only seemed fitting that he be allowed to spend as much time as possible with the dying man in his final days. Due to his exceptional record and popularity among the unit, the commander reluctantly granted the request. He hated to lose a man like Jack, but given the situation, he felt there was little choice.

Jack's departure from his unit and his friends in Panama had been hard, but knowing where he was going and why was even harder. In his heart he'd always known that this day was coming. Over the past few months, letters from his mother and Rich had described Charlie's worsening condition. It had been Jack's mother, Claire, who, through threats, intimidation and finally tears, managed to get Charlie into a doctor's office. Their worst fears had proven to be right. Charlie had cancer and it was inoperable. Charlie had waited far too long. He was dying and there was nothing they could do.

His transfer to Bragg completed, Jack immediately went home on leave. His mother had tried to prepare her son for their first visit to see Charlie, but nothing she had said could have prepared the battle-hardened ranger for the sight that greeted him that day.

At first, Jack thought there had to be a mistake. They must have had the wrong room. The frail-looking, bald-headed man with the sunken eyes and cheekbones couldn't be Charlie. But it was and the initial shock tore at young Jack's heart. It was all he could do to keep from falling all apart right there. Part of him wanted to be brave and strong for Charlie, while another part of him wanted to break down and cry like a baby at the sight that lay so frail and helpless before him.

A flood of memories flashed through Jack's mind at that moment. Memories of a caring, loving bear of a man, tossing a young boy into the air and catching him, all the while smiling that broad, almost devilish, grin of his. The sight of bulging muscles, rippling along huge arms as strong hands lifted transmissions and moved massive auto parts that should have taken two men; watching the glint in his eyes as he tossed back a beer and talked of racing and cars; the country boy smile and backwoods laugh that always seem to win people over and put them at ease; a man who wholeheartedly believed that a man's word was better and more binding than all the contracts that had ever been written. That was the Charlie Kincade

Jack pictured in his mind as he bent over the bed and kissed the sleeping man gently on the forehead.

Charlie's eyes fluttered open for a moment. His breathing was hard and labored, but he managed a smile and the eyes seemed to brighten when they realized that it was Jack standing there. It was a look full of pride and love. Jack ran his hand lightly over Charlie's head as he whispered, "I'm here, Charlie. I love you."

Jack could see tears welling up in his uncle's eyes.

"You don't worry about anything, Charlie. You can beat this thing. I know you can."

Reaching down, he clasped Charlie's trembling hand as he continued, "You got to get better, Charlie. You know I can't drive without you there to chew on my ass once and awhile."

Charlie smiled once more, squeezing Jack's hand with what little strength he had. He winked at the boy, then his eyes closed and he drifted off into another deep sleep. Jack held his hand for a long time, then quietly left the room.

Rich was waiting for Jack out in the hallway.

"How is he?" Rich asked.

"Sleeping, I think. God, he looks so bad, Rich," said Jack with a deep-felt sigh.

Rich only nodded. He had been with his brother throughout the entire ordeal. The chemotherapy, the radiation, the experimental drugs. But in the end, nothing was working. There was little he could say. He had accepted that there was nothing he or anyone else could do now. Having Jack home helped ease the pain of that reality. It was only a matter of time before it would be over.

That time came one week later. Rich called Jack in the middle of the night. Charlie had never regained consciousness. Jack had been the last person he'd seen before he died. After having hung up the phone that night, Jack had gone out on the front porch steps and sat. He remained there until just before dawn. Now there were only memories. As the sun rose, Jack wept for the loss of an uncle, a father, and the closest and dearest friend he'd ever had.

The funeral service was held a few days later. A huge crowd attended. Judge Harting was there and Tyrell took leave from Fort Benning to attend. That night Jack, Rich and Tyrell went to a local bar and drank a considerable amount in honor of Charlie Kincade. Afterward, they went to a restaurant for breakfast. While they were waiting for their order, Tyrell asked, "What'll you do now, Rich? I mean, you going to take over the garage?"

Rich lit a smoke, "I suppose I'll have to, Tyrell. Charlie left me fifty percent of the business in his will. The other half went to Willa May and the kids. But hell, none of them want anything to do with the place. Jack's the only one of the kids that ever showed any interest in motors and cars. I imagine they'll be pressing their mom to sell the place or for me to buy her out. They don't care for that kind of work, but they'll sure as hell want the money it'll bring, you can count on that."

"What about the cars and all the racing equipment?" asked Jack.

Rich smiled. "Oh, yeah. Guess I forgot to tell you, didn't I? Charlie left all that stuff to you and me, fifty-fifty. The cars, the haulers, equipment—everything. The kids want to sell the place, that's fine. But all that stuff belongs to us, no matter which way it goes."

"You going to buy her out?" asked Jack.

Rich stared out the window for a moment, then answered, "I don't know, Jack. I'll be sixty years old before long. That's a little late in life to be taking on a business that big. I never really cared much for the paperwork and office stuff. Not that good with figures an' all.

Charlie took care of that end. I guess I was just really into it for the racing more than anything else."

"How much you figure the place is worth, Rich?" asked Tyrell.

Rich thought about that for a minute then said, "Well, Charlie ran eighty-five thousand dollars worth of business through there last year, and that was after everything had been paid, including that damn, blood-sucking IRS."

Jack was stunned by the figure Rich had just quoted. He'd never realized how much money was involved in the business until now. But then, when he thought about it, Charlie had built the place on a solid reputation for quality work that was guaranteed. Over the years that reputation garnered him not only repeat clientele, but plenty of business from the large, high-volume dealerships as well.

Jack and Tyrell were looking at one another across the table. It was clear they were both thinking the same thing. It was also a look that hadn't gone unnoticed by Rich, who asked, "Just what are we thinkin' about here, boys?"

Tyrell grinned. "What'd you think, Jack. Could we do it?"

"I wonder," came the reply.

Rich nodded his approval. Although they hadn't said it yet, Rich knew where they were headed.

"You just want to buy my half or the whole thing?" he asked.

The two rangers were still looking at each other.

"The whole thing," said Jack. "How much you figure, Rich?"

Rich threw his hands up, "Wooo-hoss! You askin' the wrong fellow. I wouldn't have any idea. But I can find out from Charlie's accountant and his lawyer. Let you know in a week or so. You boys serious about this?"

They both nodded in agreement.

"What about the army?"

"Not a problem," said Tyrell. "We both came in the army the same time—we'll both be getting out at the same time next year."

The waitress was doing a balancing act with their breakfast plates as she headed for their table as Rich said, "Okay, then. I'll get all the information and figures rounded up and we'll see where we stand in a few days. Reckon I could run the place until you boys get out of the service. I think Charlie would have liked the idea. Yes, sir. I really do."

Jack and Tyrell smiled across the table at each other, then reaching out, shook hands. "Screw that workin' for somebody else. Right, partner?" said Jack.

"Right on, brother."

Passing the plates around the table, the waitress remarked, "You boys hear the news? We just invaded Panama."

15

The Panama War had been one of short duration and one that would earn no more than a few pages in the history books. But it had served to get both Tyrell and Jack recalled off leave status. No sooner had the Panama situation calmed down, when out of nowhere, trouble blew up in the Middle East. Iraq invaded Kuwait and unlike Panama, where few people took notice, or even cared, suddenly the world was fixed on the little country of Kuwait . . . and why? Because they weren't talking about drug money or bananas this time; this was serious—this was about oil.

To Jack the entire world seemed to be going nuts. Everybody wanted to fight and the U.S. was right in the middle of the whole thing. They just didn't seem to understand. All he wanted to do was finish his enlistment and go back home to run a garage and race cars. There wasn't anything in that plan that suggested any type of desert war, jungle war, or even a damn cold war.

Luckily for Jack there was an admin clerk at Fort Bragg that was on the ball. The day the rangers were alerted for deployment to the Middle East, the clerk noticed that Jack's enlistment would be up in less than four months and brought that information to the attention of the unit commander.

They immediately called Jack in and offered him just about anything and everything to reenlist on the spot. There was actually a moment when Jack gave the idea serious consideration. He liked the army, the rangers, and the quality people he worked and served with. But he also knew that if he signed up for another hitch, he'd never leave. He'd be destined to become a twenty-year man. A "lifer" just like Deke. The moment of consideration vanished, being overridden by the lure of fast cars and steep-banked tracks which seem to be calling him back. He would leave the army and the rangers, but he'd still have his own wars—only they'd be fought at places with names like Darlington, Talladega, Daytona, and Atlanta Speedway. No, he'd never regret his time in the military, but it was now time to move on with his life. Three months, two weeks and one day later, Jack did just that. He left Fort Bragg for the last time and headed home. His first stop was Judge Harting's courtroom. His military career was over and his police record in the state of North Carolina no longer existed.

Rich had managed to broker a deal to buy the remaining fifty percent of the business, but it hadn't come cheap. Willa May proved that she hadn't only been a good wife to Charlie, but a very attentive one as well when it came to money. She was fully aware of the yearly income from the business and as such, had used those numbers to set her price of $300,000. Rich had almost had a heart attack on the spot when he heard her price. He reminded her that Charlie's life insurance alone was enough to keep her and the kids more than comfortable for a long time, and besides, this was Jack, whom she had always loved as a son, who was wanting to buy the place. Not somebody they didn't even know. This final argument touched the mother instinct in Willa May—but only $50,000 dollars worth, dropping her price to $250,000 dollars. Rich considered telling her what kind of a mother he thought she was, but then thought better of it out of respect for Charlie and agreed on the price.

Rich had found a bank to go the loan and hold the paper on the business. Tyrell and Jack both had a total of thirty thousand dollars they had saved over their three years in the service and kicked that in the pot. Tyrell's father had been disappointed at first that his son wouldn't be coming home to take over for him, but he also understood what an opportunity this was for Tyrell. The night he had left, his father wished him well in his venture and gave him a check for $10,000.

The first few months, things went so well that hardly anyone noticed the change. Jack, Rich, and Tyrell divided their time between the garage work and getting the cars ready for the upcoming racing season. Rich also had the task of teaching Tyrell everything he knew about racing, but luckily, Tyrell was a quick learner. After less than three months of track time, he could run side by side with Rich or Jack, and occasionally, he actually beat them in practice runs.

Rich was still considered the owner and manager of the place and he had solved his paperwork problem by hiring what he considered to be a highly knowledgeable and capable office staff, along with a twenty-five-year-old business major fresh out of North Carolina State, by the name of Brian Wells, to oversee the entire operation. He was personable, intelligent, and highly ambitious, often working long into the night after everyone else had gone home. Rich figured the boy was trying to impress him and never gave the matter another thought.

By mid-February owners and drivers were working

and reworking their cars, getting them prepared for the first race of the year, which would be held at the Atlanta Speedway to kickoff the 1991 season. The Kincade team set up three cars to start the season. But for the first time in twenty-five years, Rich wouldn't be driving any of them. Like he had told the boys at the outset, he was gettin' "far too old and way too slow" to be matching gas pedals with boys their age. He'd work the spotter position and handle communications. That'd keep him busy.

As race day drew near, everything seemed to be going well. The cars were running perfect and in timed trials, Woody's pit crew had actually managed to cut a few seconds off their time from the previous year. Confidence was running high among the members of the Kincade Racing Team.

To say that the sudden appearance of Federal Agent Mark Jackson at the front door of the garage was a major letdown would be a total understatement. Tyrell was the first to notice the fleet of unmarked cars and a black van speeding into the parking lot.

"Now, what the hell is that all about?" he asked.

Rich and Jack pulled their heads out from under the hood of a car they were working on and saw Jackson standing in the doorway.

"Jesus, I wonder what that prick wants?" said Jack, wiping his hands on a shop rag.

"Don't know," muttered Rich, "but you can bet it's not to talk about old times."

Within seconds a swarm of armed agents in flak jackets burst past Jackson and, with their weapons pointed at everyone in the garage area, began yelling for everyone to get flat on the floor. Tyrell glanced over and asked, "What's happening here, Jack?"

"Just do what they say, Tyrell. This guy's a real hard ass. He'd like nothing better than to bust our heads."

"Everybody do as they say," yelled Rich.

"Wise advice, Mr. Kincade," said Jackson as he moved forward and stood over the trio on the floor. Smiling down at Jack, the agent continued, "Told you we'd meet again, didn't I, Jack."

"Area's all secure, sir!" yelled someone from the back of the garage.

"Very well. Start the search."

Tapping Rich's leg with the point of his shoe, Jackson asked, "You are the primary owner and operator of this business, is that correct, Mr. Kincade?"

"You damn well know I am," snarled Rich. "An' I suppose you got a warrant for this shit, right?"

"Of course I do. All three of you get on your feet," commanded Jackson.

It was all Jack could do to keep from reaching out and grabbing the son of a bitch by the throat. But that wouldn't help anything or anybody at the moment. Instead, he barked, "Just what the hell is this, Jackson?"

The agent placed the warrants in Rich's hand, then with a smug look on his face and a hint of pleasure in his voice, he said, "Mr. Kincade. You are under arrest for violation of the federal drug laws of the United States, and charged with the distribution and selling of cocaine. All property and assets are hereby confiscated and will remain the possession of the Federal Government until released or sold at public auction in accordance with the rules of the Drug Compensation Act."

Jackson finished his little speech by reading Rich his rights while the handcuffs were being put on and he was led away to a car which immediately left for the federal courthouse. A few minutes later, agents brought Brian Wells down the stairs and did the same thing with him.

Another agent stepped up to Jackson. "Sir, we found close to one hundred pounds of coke in the door panels of a Chevy and a Ford truck. We're pretty sure there's more scattered around the place."

"Fine," said Jackson. "Have them bring in the dogs and check it all."

Jack was furious. "And just who the hell is supposed to be doing all this drug dealing, Mr. Jackson?"

"Oh, there's no, 'supposed' about it, Jack." Jackson smiled. "We've got it all on videotape. Your Mr. Wells and his friends have been moving some major drugs out of this place nearly every night for the last three months. We got tape, dates, times and places. It's a rock-solid case, Jack. No fuckups this time."

Tyrell asked, "You got Rich Kincade on that tape of yours, agent man?"

The smile dropped from Jackson's smug face. Now it was Jack's turn to grin.

"You don't do you? That's because Rich wouldn't be involved in anything like this and you know it. Hell, he would have called you himself if he'd known what Wells was doing. And you know that too, you prick!"

"Doesn't really matter, now," said Jackson. "Under the new law, all property and assets become ours until such time as a verdict is rendered in the case. That's the law, boys. So you see it really doesn't matter if Rich was dealing or not. His place of business and a number of his employees were."

"Just exactly what does that mean in English?" asked Tyrell.

"That means we slap a lock on this place and everything in or around it is the property of the U.S. government," said Jackson, with a satisfied look on his face.

Jack took a threatening step forward as he yelled, "You know this is bullshit, Jackson. You've made this a personal thing, you son of a bitch!"

Jackson took a step back. "Now Jack, you don't want to do anything stupid. Your uncle and Wells are the only two I have warrants for, but I could damn well add one more if you feel the urge to assault a federal officer."

Tyrell grabbed Jack's arm before he could swing.

"Ain't worth it, Jack. We got enough problems right now without this crap, okay!"

Jack backed off. Tyrell was right. They had one hell of a problem. Every dime they had was tied up in the garage and the race cars. If Jackson was right, they had just lost their total sources of income for who knew how long. The cars and the equipment were being logged and tagged as they stood there. The Kincade Garage and the Kincade Racing Team no longer existed. Yeah, they definitely had a major problem.

Two hours later, Jack and Tyrell stood in the parking lot watching the last of the federal agents drive away.

"God, I'm glad Charlie wasn't here to see this," said Jack.

"Yeah, me too," said Tyrell. "I'm afraid they would have had to shoot him dead before they put a lock on that door." Tyrell paused a moment, then asked, "Any idea what we're going to do next?"

Jack shook his head. "Not really. I'm going to make a call to Judge Harting. He's a federal judge. If anybody knows a way around this, he will. Why don't you go on home, Tyrell. I'll give you a call later. Let you know where we stand."

Tyrell agreed. There really wasn't anything else he could do, but wait. "Later, man."

Jack sat on the fender of his car staring at the padlocked door. Jesus, what were they going to do? It was a good bet that Jackson's warrants and the arrest and confiscation were all legal as hell. The guy had been burnt once by the Kincades; in a way, that was what this was all about. The odds that he'd made a mistake were zero to none. What really made it aggravating was the fact that neither Rich, nor anyone else knew what that hot-shot college stud had been doing all this time. Jackson knew that was a fact, but because he felt he'd been embarrassed in Harting's courtroom three years ago, he was going to make the Kincades pay. Oh, sure. After a full investigation and a grand jury hearing, Rich would be exonerated of any wrong-doing, but that could take anywhere from six months to over a year. What were they supposed to do in the meantime? All of a sudden, a life as a ranger didn't seem all that difficult.

Judge Harting confirmed what Jack had suspected. Jackson had done his job well. He'd followed procedure to the letter on the warrants and the search. He'd left nothing to chance. The call hadn't been a total loss. The judge agreed to move Rich's arraignment to the top of the list and guarantee bail just in case Jackson had any ideas of declaring Rich a flight risk.

Harting apologized for not being able to do more, but Jackson actually had a solid case this time. And even though Rich had not been involved with the drugs, the garage had been, causing it to fall under the new law. After the trial they could file an appeal, but there were no guarantees and the process was a long and expensive one to pursue.

Jack thanked Harting for his help and advice. Hanging up the phone, he slumped back in his chair. Just like that, it was all gone. Charlie's thirty-five years of hard work, Rich's retirement, and practically every cent he and Tyrell had to their name—all gone. And for something they had nothing to do with.

Jack's next call was to Tyrell, who could tell by the sound of Jack's voice that the news was going to be bad—all bad. And he was right.

Two days later they were in Judge Harting's courtroom for Rich's arraignment. Just as Harting had figured, Jackson objected to the idea of bail. But he was quickly overruled by his favorite judge. The bail was set at a staggering $200,000 dollars, primarily because it was drug-related and involved distribution. When North Carolina said they had zero tolerance for drug dealers, they meant just that.

Jack's mother put up her house to cover part of the bail and Willa May covered the rest of it. By that afternoon, Tyrell, Jack and Rich were sitting on Rich's front porch having a beer and still searching for an answer to their problem, but it didn't look good.

"Guess I should have kept a closer eye on the business," said Rich. "That damn kid wouldn't have put that shit over on Charlie. My brother was a lot smarter than folks gave him credit for. No, Sir. Charlie would have smelled a rat before the thing ever got that far."

"Can't blame yourself, Rich. He had us all fooled," said Tyrell.

"Shit! You know what really pisses me off?" snapped Rich. "I kept seeing the damn kid workin' late nearly every night and was thinking I ought to give him a damn raise for the fine work he was doin' . . . figured he could use a little extra money. Hell! Them feds found over one hundred thousand dollars in his damn bedroom alone. Ain't that a kick in the balls."

Jack couldn't help but laugh and it quickly became contagious. They were all three still laughing when they heard the rumble of a semi coming around the mountain road that passed just beyond Rich's front yard fence. It was a huge thing, a double-decker, done up in bright silver and black. A huge picture of a bright yellow Ford Thunderbird, with a number 31 painted on the car, covered the side panel of the semi-trailer.

"That's Hudy Bowlin, from up near Crawford. Must be on his way to Atlanta. Damn near took me an Charlie out of the runnin' couple of years ago with that yellow bird of his."

Jack recognized the name. "That the same Hudy Bowlin that used to run the dirt track over at Collinsville with an old beat up Plymouth, seven–eight years ago?"

"Sure enough," said Rich. "Same boy."

"Seems to be doing a lot better these days," said Jack. "That hauler alone must cost about fifty thousand dollars."

Rich chuckled, "More like seventy-five thousand dollars. Once Hudy started winning races, he found himself a couple of high-profile sponsors about two years ago. Better car, better crew, and solid equipment makes all the difference in this business, boys. You see, Hudy always was a good driver, he just needed a top-of-the-line ride. Ever since he got one, he's been finishing in the top twenty-five on the money charts. Even made it on television a few times last year."

Tyrell opened another beer and leaned back as he said, "That's what we need, Jack. A high-profile sponsor."

Rich shook his head. "Not as easy as all that, son. First you got to show 'em you can drive. Put together a winning record, or at least plenty of decent finishes in some big-name races. A sponsor's not going to lay out the kind of money it takes to keep a car on the track if the only people that are going to see his logo are two or three hundred good ol' boys in Flatbush. I know what I'm talkin' about there. Me and Charlie first got started we couldn't find any big name to back us, and brother it's a tough go out there for an independent. Hell, with tires costin' up to six-hundred-fifty dollars a set and a fellow knowin' he's gonna' need at least two sets for backup at a place like Darlington or Nashville, he better be winnin' a lot or have a hell of a good paying day job. Then you got the fuel, spare parts, communications gear and a crew that knows what they're doin' and that's just the stuff you have to have every week on the circuit. Throw in the unexpected and a good crash every now and then that almost totals your ride and you get an idea what it costs to run one race. Took Charlie and me ten years of hard-ass work before we could afford our first new car and keep it outfitted for just one season.

"No, sir, son. It takes a wad of cash, along with your name and picture in the papers or on the tube, and often, to draw the big fish. They see those pictures and imagine what their logo would look like on that car or the driver's jumpsuit, being seen by thousands or even millions. That's what they'll pay for. Yes, sir."

Tyrell had listened carefully to Rich and as interesting as he found the conversation, it only served to depress him even more. Who was going to put up that kind of money to back a couple of ex-army rangers. Especially one that had never run a real race and another that had only driven in a few amateur races over the last three years . . . and he hadn't won any of those. Without the garage, the cars and the equipment, the entire conversation was no more than an exercise in futility.

Jack had been silent throughout Rich's discussion, listening to every word. Then, like a bolt from the blue, he suddenly knew what he had to do. Jumping to his feet, Jack headed across the yard to his car.

"Hey, where you goin' Jack?" shouted Tyrell.

Jack turned and replied, "I'm going to Dallas, Texas. Don't do anything until I get back."

Rich looked over at Tyrell. "Did he say, Dallas, Texas?"

Watching the black Trans Am back out of the yard, Tyrell took another hit off his beer before he said, "Yeah. Dallas, Texas. Any idea why he'd go to Texas?"

Rich shook his head. "Nope. You want another beer? It could be a long wait."

16

Rich fumbled around in the dark for the ringing phone.

"Hello . . . hello."

"Rich! Sorry to wake you, but when's that first amateur qualifier?"

"Jack . . . Jack, is that you? What time is it? Where you at?"

"It's about three in the morning, Rich. Now listen. When is that first race?"

Rich tried to clear his head a moment, then answered, "Nine days from now at Atlanta. Why?"

There was that old familiar ring of excitement in Jack's voice as he said, "Okay. Tomorrow . . . or I should say, today, I want you and Tyrell to scout around the dealerships for two brand-new cars to put on a track. Make one a Ford T-Bird and whatever you think best for the second. Next get in touch with Woody Clark. Have him get the team together. I want them to hit all the speed shops and get everything we'd need to set up a complete racing garage. Computers, spare parts, balancers, the works. If it's in stock, have them set it aside and tell 'em we'll pick it up in twenty-four hours. And don't forget the tires—lots of tires. At least five sets for each car. That should get us started."

Rich was wide awake now and trying to keep up with Jack's list of things to do.

"Next, check out the area for a hauler. See if anybody's got one for sale. If not, get the price on a new one. Have Tyrell lay on the communications gear, racing suits, helmets and whatever other gear we'll need."

Jack finally paused a moment, then asked, "Have I forgot anything, Rich?"

Before Rich could answer, Jack was back on the line. "Well, if I did, I'm sure you'll think of it, Rich. I'll be back in Charlotte by tonight. Call Tyrell and tell him we're back in the racin' business. That should make his day. Gotta' run, Rich. See you guys tonight. Bye."

Before Rich could say a word there was a click on the line and Jack was gone. Pulling himself out of bed, he made his way to the kitchen, started a pot of coffee. Grabbing a pen and paper he began to write down the list of things he was supposed to do—it was a long list. When he had finished, he called Tyrell, who asked the same question about the time.

"Don't ask," said Rich. He then told Tyrell about Jack's call and what he wanted them to do. By the time Rich was finished, Tyrell asked, "He didn't sound drunk or anything, did he?"

Rich assured him that the only thing Jack was high on was excitement. He'd explain it all when he got in from Dallas, but in the meantime, they had a lot of work to do. Rich would be by to pick him up at around eight. They'd have breakfast and start hitting the dealerships looking for cars.

Tyrell was silent for a second, then Rich asked, "You don't think that kid robbed a bank or something, do you, Tyrell?"

"No, nothing like that, Rich."

"How can you be so damn sure?"

Tyrell laughed, "Because if he had, you'd have that ass, Jackson, sittin' in your lap right now. See you at eight."

17

It was a nervous group that was waiting in Rich's kitchen when Jack finally arrived at the house. He was all smiles as he came through the door and greeted them with a big grin. Stacked in the center of the table were a pile of order forms and receipts from a busy day. Tyrell reached into the icebox and pulled out a six-pack of beer. Setting it on the table, he said, "Okay, magic boy. Tell us a story."

Reaching inside his shirt pocket, Jack withdrew a piece of paper and placed it in the center of the table. Pulling a beer from the pack, he sat back to watch their expressions. For a minute no one did anything but stare at the piece of paper. Then Jack said, "Go on, Rich. Have a look at it."

Rich reached out and picked up the once folded paper. Opening it up, he couldn't believe what he was reading. It was a contract between the Kincade Racing Team and Ward Industries. Attached to the contract was a check for two hundred and fifty thousand dollars. Rich couldn't speak. His mouth had gone dry. He passed the paper over to Tyrell, who let out a yell. "Holy shit, Jack! That's a quarter of a million bucks! How'd you pull it off?"

"Remember me telling you about that little action down in Colombia? Well, that's the guy. Ross Ward. He wanted to just give me the money, but that didn't seem right. I didn't go down there looking for a handout. I went with a business deal in mind. The Ward organization is now the official sponsor of the Kincade Racing Team. That's our first installment. If we need more, all we have to do is call. Now, how'd you guys do with getting things together?"

No one answered. They were still in shock. The check had worked its way around to Woody, who held it as if it were a rare piece of art work.

"Do we even have any cars to drive in a race?" asked Jack.

Suddenly everyone was trying to talk. There was an air of excitement in the room. They were going to be racing this year, regardless of Agent Jackson and his bullshit.

With only eight days before the Atlanta race, everyone had a hundred things to do. The first order of business was moving everything into another garage that Woody had leased for them. It hadn't been used in over a year, but came with everything they'd need to set up operations. Rich had picked up a '91 Ford T-Bird and a '91 Pontiac Grand Prix. Woody and his crew were already installing the roll bars and safety equipment, while Jack and Tyrell were making some modifications on the car hauler Rich had brought. Everyone was busy and they worked well into the night, but no one was complaining. They were back in business and that was all that mattered.

With the race only five days away, Woody called his brother-in-law, who just happened to work in operations at the Charlotte Motor Speedway. After a short conversation and threats about exposing certain indiscretions with a few bar girls that Woody knew, they managed to get the use of the Speedway for test-running the cars the following day.

Rich and Woody kept the times. Jack set a blistering pace with the T-Bird, while Tyrell's was respectable, but it was obvious he was still unsure of himself, and far too timid when it came to pushing the big Pontiac to its maximum potential. On the ride back to the garage, Rich mentioned this fact to Jack. Tyrell was a good kid, but he was driving scared and you couldn't win races that way. You had to be willing to take risks. Jack was aware of the problem, but felt that the more races Tyrell ran, the more comfortable he'd become with the track and the car. He was sure the ex-ranger had the right stuff for the fast track—he just needed some time.

Rich muttered something under his breath. Jack glanced over at him. "What are you muttering about?"

Rich slumped back in the seat and crossed his arms. "I said he's got plenty of time . . . like three days!"

"You're sure hard on a guy, Rich."

"Hey, this sport is called racing, Jack. That means speed. Speed—that's what wins races. No sense in puttin' a damn car together to do a hundred and fifty if you're just gonna' drive it to church on Sunday."

Jack laughed. "Oh, that was a good one, Rich. Don't worry, I know Tyrell's got what it takes. He'll get it together, you'll see."

The following morning they were helping Woody and the crew load up the cars and equipment into the hauler, when Claire came driving up. She had been to town. Their postman had seen her and gave her a box addressed to Jack. It was from Dallas, Texas. As they all gathered around, Jack opened the package. Inside were a multitude of colorful logos, stencils, and decals, all representing Ward Industries products. Included were two black hats with the word RANGER printed across the front in bold gold lettering. Along with the hats came a note. "Best Wishes and Good Luck, Rangers—Airborne!" signed, Ross and Karen Ward.

Woody and the boys had gotten the logos on the cars during the night and made a few final checks on the engines before they went to bed. Rich was already asleep in the hauler, but Jack and Tyrell were both too nervous for that. They had walked around to the side entrance to the stands and made their way to the top of the bleachers. From there they had a complete view of the entire track and the infield, which was already crammed full of RV's and campers. There were still a few barbecue grills glowing in the darkness and with the camper lights still on, it almost seemed like a small city surrounded by a ring of cold, gray concrete and asphalt.

Tyrell lit a cigarette.

"Didn't know you smoked," said Jack.

"Used to do it a lot. Guess I'm just nervous."

Jack knew the feeling well. "You'll do fine, Tyrell. Just remember everything Rich taught you, listen to what he says on the radio and go with your gut instincts."

"Yeah, that's about what Rich said earlier."

Tyrell took another puff of his cigarette and let the smoke out slowly before he said, "Jack, you, Rich, Woody and the crew—you've all been great to me. I want to thank you for that."

Jack glanced over at his friend. "Are we gettin' all sentimental here or what?"

Tyrell shook his head. "Naw, nothing like that. It's just that, well, where I come from, black folks aren't treated all that well by the white majority. You know what I mean?"

"Yeah, I think I do. And by the way—if you want to be politically correct, it's African Americans, not blacks."

Tyrell grinned, "Hell, whatever they're calling us now.

Fact is we're still black. Guess what I'm trying to say is, you all make me feel comfortable . . . kind of like one of the family, and I appreciate that, Jack. I really do. But you know, I haven't seen a hell of a lot of black drivers in this game."

Jack slapped him on the leg. "Hey, you are one of the family and don't you forget it. Anybody messes with you, they mess with us all. You ever hear of a guy named Wendell Scott?"

Tyrell shook his head. "No, can't say I have."

"Well, Wendell was a black driver. Ran moonshine out of Danville, Virginia. Only full-time black driver in NASCAR history. Ran the circuit for twelve years, from nineteen sixty-one to nineteen seventy-three. Out of five hundred races, he only won one."

"No shit," said Tyrell. "I didn't know that. He only won one race in all that time?"

"Yeah, but he lined up for five hundred—that's the point. He wouldn't be intimidated or allow himself to feel threatened. An I don't have to tell you how things were in the sixties, I'm sure you know better than I do. But, Tyrell, what Wendell did back then took a lot of guts. I think you've got that same spirit. You can pick up where Wendell left off. I know you can."

Flipping the cigarette away, Tyrell replied, "Oh, yeah, how? You're talking NASCAR. We're just running amateur stuff here, Jack."

"You've got to start at the bottom in this business, Tyrell. But there's nothing that says you've got to stay there. We start winning often enough and somebody's going to take notice. That's how we work our way up to the big time. But we can't let them intimidate us, Tyrell. We've got to show them we can run with the best of 'em. That means going all out. No holding back. We push it to the edge, then some. We take the risk and the chances, whatever it takes to win. Can you do that Tyrell? Are you willing to put your ass on the line?"

Tyrell was laughing as he answered, "God damn, Jack! You'd have made one hell of a football coach, you know that? Well send me in coach—I'm ready!"

18

The set-up for the Atlanta race was going to be different from the earlier races Jack had run. This was actually a dual event, with the big boys from NASCAR's Winston Cup being the prime-time event on Sunday. The amateur race, tagged the Sears 150, was a ninety-six-mile race scheduled for Saturday night. It would draw an estimated twenty-one thousand fans and paid out $30,000 dollars. A mere drop in the bucket compared to the 1.5 million the big boys would be running for Sunday, but like Jack said, you had to start somewhere.

Another rule change had done away with the drawing of numbers for position. Now, each driver was required to run for qualifying time and that time determined his position in the lineup. That hadn't been a problem for Jack, who had run well enough to earn himself a number-five position on the pole. Tyrell on the other hand, was still holding back on the Pontiac, something that sent Rich's blood pressure to near the boiling point. But Jack still refused to allow the ol' veteran driver to say anything to him about it. Tyrell had ended up at number twenty-one on the outside . . . four cars short of last place.

The moment of truth was at hand. There was a total of fifty glimmering cars of all makes, models and colors following the pace car around the big oval. Fans lined the roofs of their RV's and campers on the infield, while those in the stands brought up their binoculars or searched their scanners to monitor the conversations of the drivers and their spotters. The low rumbling sound of the cars began to increase as they came out of the third turn and the pace car picked up speed. Rich was on the radio, "Okay boys, this looks like it could be a good start. Get ready."

As the double line of cars uncoiled out of the turn like some wide, colorful snake, the starter, perched high on the overhanging catwalk, stood with the green flag held above his head and looked the field over. Satisfied that they had good position, the pace car was alerted and it immediately accelerated and swung off the track onto pit row. At the same time, Rich saw the flag coming down. "It's a good start! Go! Go! Go!" The low rumble now became a loud roar as fifty V-8 engines made their presence known to the people of Atlanta.

In a mad scramble, cars were shooting to the outside and passing anyone they could before the first turn. Jack hung onto his position on the inside, staying right on the rear of the number-three car. Tyrell had followed Rich's instructions and swung up on the high side in an attempt to move up in the pack, but he couldn't or wouldn't hold it. Seeing the turn quickly approaching, he dropped back down into the slot, a move that cost him. He was now running in thirty-eighth place.

Jack was satisfied to hold what he had for the first ten laps in order to study the movements of the cars in front of him. During this time, Tyrell had decided it was time he made a move and fought his way up to twenty-fifth position.

By the eighteenth lap, Jack let Rich know that he was going to make a move on turn two. The third-place car was drifting in the curves. If Jack timed it right and the T-Bird had the punch he thought it did, he'd have between two to four seconds to close the gap on the inside and leave the three car high and dry on the outside. Rich agreed with him. As they went into the turn, the other driver did exactly what Jack had expected and began to drift up out of the slot.

"Now, Jack! Hit it! Hit it!" shouted Rich over the radio. "You've got him! Get in there, boy! Close it up!"

The T-Bird leaped forward just enough so that when they came out of the turn, the number-three car didn't have anywhere to go. By having to stay high, he actually dropped back four positions in the pack. Jack was now in sole possession of third place. The crowd loved it and roared their approval.

The battle continued for another ten laps before the inevitable happened. One of the rookies from the back of the pack came roaring along the high side near the wall in an attempt to pass on a turn, but he had too much speed for the angle coming out of the turn and lost it. Sliding into a spin, he took out two cars below him and sent a third sideways, which was immediately hit broadside by two others. It was a total mess. Tires exploded and loose metal and oil went all over the track, sending cars scrambling to dodge the debris and damaged cars. Rich was shouting into the headset at Tyrell. "Stay high, Tyrell. Stay high. You've got metal in the middle of the track. Back it off—back off! That's it. Okay, you're clear. Both of you, bring 'em in for fuel. We've got time right now."

Woody and his crew were all over both cars seconds before they had come to a complete stop. Water bottles were shoved at the drivers while fuel tanks were filled and tires checked. Everything checked out okay. Within thirty seconds, both cars were heading back onto the track, taking their positions while still cruising under the yellow caution flag.

A total of eleven cars had been eliminated from the race. That left thirty-nine still chasing the money and victory. Jack still held his third-place position and Tyrell had managed to move up to fifteenth place, thanks to the pile-up. The next twenty-five laps became a cat and mouse game, with drivers trying to bait each other out of position, or attempting to intimidate competitors with a little bump here or a nudge there on the curves, in the hopes of shaking them up enough to force them out of their way. For a few it worked, but not many.

Another crash at lap sixty put seven more cars out of the running and four more had blown engines or overheated and had to pull out of the running. By lap one hundred there were only twenty-eight cars left on the track. Jack and Tyrell were still hanging in there, with Jack holding a solid grip on third and Tyrell having eased himself up into the number-twelve position. Rich kept trying to get Tyrell to move up. The two cars in front of him were starting to get careless and were swinging high on the curves, leaving the slot open for Tyrell, if only he'd make the move. But so far, he wasn't listening to Rich, apparently satisfied with where he was.

At the 120 mark, Jack had decided he had stared at the rear end of the number-two Chevy long enough. It was time to do something. There were only thirty laps left and he still hadn't had a chance to make a run at the leader.

"Rich, have you been watching the number-two man?" asked Jack.

"Roger—all the way, Jack."

"You seen anything I can use for an edge?"

"Negative, Jack. The guy's sittin' the saddle tight and he knows the game."

"Okay, Rich. I'm going to make a run at him on the next turn. Watch my high side."

"You got it, Jack. Don't worry about punchin' the Bird. She can take it. Good luck."

Jack inched up to the Chevy's rear and allowed the Ford to drift a little high until he was at the Chevy's right rear. As they started into the curve, Jack drifted out and took the Ford's accelerator to the floor. There was less than six inches between the two cars as they went into the turn. Slowly, the T-Bird gained on the Chevy until they were running door to door. But Jack knew he couldn't afford to back off. He'd have to pass him on this curve or he'd lose him on the straightaway.

Rich was screaming on the radio. "You've got him, Jack. Keep it down. Keep it down, son. Don't back off. Ride it out—you can do it."

Out of the corner of his eye, Jack thought he saw the Chevy shimmy a little, then suddenly, the radiator seemed to explode sending steam and water onto the windshield and over the top of the number-two car. It swerved slightly to the right, hitting Jack's left rear panel, then went into a 360-spin toward the infield. At the moment of impact, Jack felt the rear of the T-Bird begin to slip to the right.

Rich was on again. "Hold it, Jack! Hold it! Don't let her get away from you. Hook right, but don't force it. Hook right."

Jack hooked the wheel right, slightly, catching the center groove of the track and the T-Bird straightened herself out just as it came onto the straightaway. Jack's heart was pounding as he whispered into the mike, "Thanks, Rich."

"Hey, that's what we're here for. You've got second place. Hold on to it. Catch your breath and in a little while, we'll make a run at the leader. You're doing great, Jack."

The Chevy had made it to the infield and clear of the track, eliminating any need for a caution flag. But it had caused enough diversion for Tyrell to sneak past two more cars and move into tenth place. Still, Rich felt he could do better. Figuring he'd been silent long enough, he said, "Hey, Tyrell. You afraid you're gonna hurt that big ass Pontiac, or what? You've been babying the thing for 135 laps—what'd you say we actually try racing the fuckin' thing before the night's over."

Jack heard every word and couldn't help but grin. Rich's little speech instantly reminded him of Charlie. And just like Charlie, Rich wasn't about to let up.

"Well, what'd you say there, hot-shot? You got fifteen laps to see if you can pass anybody without the help of a damn yellow flag. Come on, Tyrell! Let's see what you can do."

Jack came on the radio. "Remember our talk last night, Tyrell. One out of five hundred. I think you can do better than that. What'd you say?"

Tyrell's answer came on the next turn. Flooring the Pontiac, he swung out and around the ninth- and eighth-place cars like they weren't even there. By the time he came out of the next turn, the nose of the Pontiac was only inches from the rear of the sixth-place car.

"Now that's what I'm talkin' about, Tyrell!" shouted Rich. "She can take it—but you've got to drive her."

Waiting until they had come out of another turn, Tyrell swung out again. Hitting 135 miles an hour, he was running door to door with the sixth-place Dodge. Slowly, he gained the lead. A foot, three feet, then six feet. As the next turn approached, Rich calmly whispered, "Okay now, Tyrell. He thinks you'll back off because of the turn—don't do it. Stay right there. He'll either have to back off or hit you. Stay with him, son. It's kinda like playing chicken. Just hang in there."

The two cars roared toward the curve at 130 miles an

hour. Any minute Tyrell expected the Dodge to slam him into the wall, but it didn't happen. Rich was right. The two cars had played a high-speed game of chicken and the other guy had just blinked. The Dodge dropped back and Tyrell quickly slid into the fifth-place spot. For the first time in over fifty laps, they heard Tyrell's voice on the radio.

"Hey, Rich. Thanks."

"No need, son. You're the one doin' the drivin'. I just do the talkin'. You done good, Tyrell."

Over the last five laps of the race, Jack tried, unsuccessfully, to pass the leader four different times. Each time the leader had fought him off, leaving Jack with a second-place finish when the checkered flag came down.

Tyrell, with his newfound confidence in himself and his car, had managed to nose out the fifth-place car in a photo finish at the line. Bringing their cars into pit row, both drivers crawled out the windows to rousing cheers from Rich and the crew. If someone had just arrived they would have thought that this was the team that had won. But then they would have no way of knowing what this group had gone through just to get the race.

Wiping sweat from his face, Jack watched Tyrell take his helmet off and smile as he said, "So, that's all there is to this racin' thing, huh?"

Jack laughed, then grabbed his friend in a bear hug as he cried, "We did it, Tyrell. Two cars in the top five. Not bad, man. Not bad at all."

Rich came over and threw his arms around both of them. "Well, boys. I guess we just served notice that the Kincade Racing Team is still very much alive and kickin'."

"Amen!" they replied.

"Uh, oh," whispered Woody, as he pointed to the infield.

Two men in suits, ties and sunglasses came up to the

group. Jack recognized one of the men that had been with Jackson that day at the garage. Now what the hell did they want?

Rich asked, "Okay fellows, what's the charge this time?"

One of the men took his glasses off as he said, "No charges, Mr. Kincade. We're here investigating an assault on a federal agent."

"Oh, really," said Tyrell. "And why should that concern us?"

"The agent was Mark Jackson. He seems to think you might have had something to do with it."

"Just when did this happen?" asked Jack.

"Last night, around nine o'clock. Outside a Charlotte restaurant."

"Sorry boys. We've been here for the last seventy-two hours," said Rich.

"I know," said the agent. "We already checked and verified that. We just thought we'd check to see if you had any idea who might have done this."

Rich couldn't hide his sarcasm. "Fellow like that couldn't have a lot of people that like him, that's for damn sure. He hurt bad?"

"Broken nose, two black eyes, a tooth missing and a broken right arm. Guess you could say he got the shit beat out of him. More than likely it was some friend of that dealer, Wells."

"Sorry we can't help you," said Jack.

The agent put his glasses back on as he said, "By the way, watched you guys race tonight. You boys are good."

"Thanks."

As the federal men turned to walk away, one of them stopped and removed a piece of paper from his suit coat and handed it to Jack. "That's a description of the guy who nailed Jackson. You hear anything, we'd appreciate a call."

"Sure. Not a problem."

Rich and Tyrell were trying hard not to laugh as the two men walked away. Rich couldn't contain himself. "Outside of you two placing tonight, I can't remember when I've had better news than that. A little attitude adjustment just might do that son-of-a-bitch some good. But I really doubt it."

Tyrell was about to say something when Jack broke out in a loud laugh and cried, "I'll be damned."

"What is it, Jack?" asked Tyrell.

"Here. Read this," said Jack, holding the paper out to Tyrell, who began reading the description out loud.

"Suspect is a male Caucasian. Six foot one, two hundred pounds with red hair and Texas accent. Has an airborne tattoo on the right forearm and was last seen in the company of a large-busted blonde—identity unknown."

A grin began to spread across Tyrell's face. "You don't think . . . no, it couldn't be."

Rich was grinning now, as he shouted, "Deke!"

They all broke into a laugh.

"Justice comes in many forms," said Tyrell.

"In the company of . . . a large-busted blonde!" said Jack, laughing so hard he was about to cry.

"Wonder how he knew about Jackson?" asked Tyrell.

"I don't know. But I'll bet we'll hear the story one of these days. But for now—God bless him, wherever he is."

Two hours later they had the cars and equipment loaded and Woody and the crew had already headed home. Jack and Rich were standing at the main gate of the garage area waiting for Tyrell to bring Rich's truck around.

"You know, your dad and Charlie would've been proud of you tonight," said Rich. The hint of sadness was unmistakable in his voice.

"Yeah, I think so too, Rich. It's funny, but there were times that I felt they were in that car with me tonight."

Rich nodded as he said, "Guess they'll always be with us, Jack."

Smiling, Jack looked up at the night sky and the stars that seemed to be winking at him, as he replied, "You know they will, Rich—as long as there's fast cars, fast tracks and southern runnin'."